Published by:
Powder River Publishing LLC
1014 Black Mountain Road
Thermopolis, Wyoming 82443

I0731141

Table of Contents

Bartered for a Price

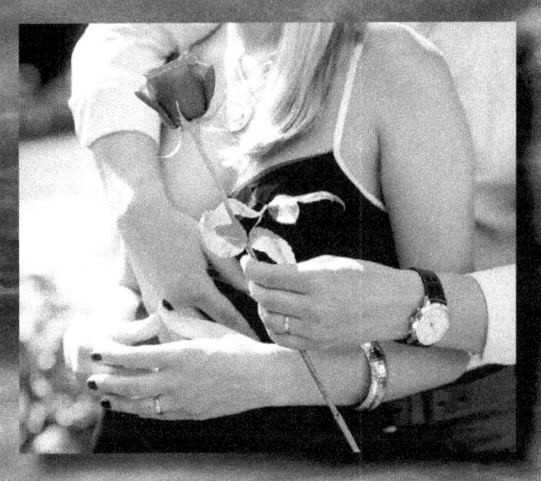

Lorine Gray

Bartered for a Price

Powder River Publishing

www.powderriverpublishing.com

Chapter 1

This wasn't happening.

Angelica Watson tucked a wayward strand of her long blond hair behind an ear, squared her shoulders, tugged the hem of her jacket straighter, and pasted on her most lethal smile.

She shifted her gaze to the massive window fronting the Buenos Aires skyline and under different circumstances she'd be admiring the view. Reflective rays cast a bright glare off the neighboring buildings. Julio Suarez's sleek, downtown offices couldn't be better situated. They were strategically centered in the city's business district. The Rio de la Plata water views glimmered in the distance. Very few people could afford this prime location.

Angelica slowly turned, her eyes locking on Simon.

She'd learned at an impressionable age to solve problems. Take control. She momentarily shut her eyes, her gut clenching with a mixture of sorrow and failure. She'd been successful before pulling them back from collapse based on her father, Simon's poor decisions. But this time was different, she'd run out of solutions.

"Angel, this is nondebatable," Simon stated, his voice invading her thoughts. He stood behind her like the tyrant he'd always been.

"Everything's negotiable," her mouth curled into a smile that didn't quite reach her lips.

"This is our last resort," Simon added, without remorse.

"Is it?" she questioned.

Her knuckles whitened as she clasped the door handle. Behind the heavy door sat the man with the finances to solve all her company's money problems. Financial juggling, over the last fiscal year, had caused her massive strain. It was getting trickier and trickier. She knew with Watson's Enterprises vulnerability seeking his help would be catastrophic. He ripped companies apart instead of save them. Simon, her often absentee father, wasn't making this any easier. Calling him dad was something she rarely did. He'd always been selfish, careless, and irresponsible. Simon's lackadaisical attitude being the exact reason she was standing in Suarez's office complex today. He'd convinced her this was the only solution for their company, but was it? She could not lose this company her family had built; despite the mess her reckless father had made of it.

The hospitality business had become her life.

She'd dropped everything to make it a success. She didn't know how to do anything else except run this chain of hotels. If they lost it, she could only walk away in abject shame. They'd be flat broke with creditors breathing down their necks. The knowledge that she had failed to protect her family's legacy didn't compare to the loss of self-respect.

Turmoil raged inside her. She'd exhausted every avenue. Angelica had been on the phone for months now, renegotiating and calling in numerous favors. It hadn't been enough.

She hated all of this. It made her sick with dread. Simon seeking resources from Suarez. The business mogul had thwarted so many of their company's financial opportunities. As if he had a vendetta against them. Suarez's company, JMS International had grown from nothing and taken over Buenos Aires' corporate real estate. His tyrannical policies had wiped out numerous competitors. Simon's insistence to involve him was still unclear to her.

Angelica's breath sliced within her lungs as her head whipped around. "Simon," she said emphatically, "Suarez isn't in the business of saving crippled companies, but dismantling them. Is that what you want?" she snapped. "To give a complete stranger control over our business."

"He's not exactly a stranger," Simon said softly so that she could barely hear him.

"What do you mean?" she asked.

Simon threw up his hand preventing any further questions. "It doesn't matter. It's irrelevant."

"What are you not telling me, Simon?" she said spitefully. "Is this another one of your disastrous secrets?" Her eyes narrowed with suspicion. "You haven't already become indebted to him? Tell me the truth," her voice dipped, "so I know all the variables before I confront Suarez."

She pinched the bridge of her nose to stem the beginning of a headache. "We need stability. This isn't some company, Simon, it's our family business. Our legacy. Our livelihood. What about the values grandfather built this company on?"

"Yes, Suarez and I have some unfinished business, but ancient history isn't part of today's business." He stared at his daughter; his jaw clenched. "Don't patronize me, Angel. Things have changed since then. Quit avoiding the unavoidable. Let's get to it."

"Really," Angelica interjected. "At least grandfather took pride in business and family," she would not back down. "Unlike you," her face reddened with agitation, "whose penchant for spending money instead of managing it has nearly destroyed everything I believe in. So, don't you dare tell me what to do." She looked at him her patience running low.

Angelica reflected back on life with her parents, Simon and Valere Watson. They'd portrayed the perfect family. The happy couple. They'd played their parts well. But Angelica had lived the truth.

Simon had discreetly enjoyed his mistresses, and Valere, she had played and dressed the perfect little society wife. Her mother, behind the scenes, had drunk a little too much wine and exercised a lot of retail therapy. She'd stayed in a horrible relationship making it work. Angelica wanted to remove the sadness from her mother's eyes before sickness had ravaged her body.

Nothing surprised her with Simon.

Simon's silver-grey hair slid down onto his brow. His matching sapphire-blue eyes battled his daughter's. "Let's not go there."

"Why not? Is it a little too close to the truth?" Her lips pursed with discontent.

The tension mounted between them. They were at a stalemate, which was often the case in their relationship.

Simon's mottled expression froze into place when the door swung inward and Angelica stood face to face with the sexiest man she'd ever seen.

. . .

Julio's heartbeat erratically dropped. The wolfish smile slid from his lips as the girl he'd banished all those years ago filled the doorway. Angelica Watson.

The hauntingly familiar face, which still somehow plagued him, was more beautiful than he remembered. He'd promised himself countless times he would never think of her in that way, ever again. But here she stood right in front of him.

"Ay, caray!" The curse slipped from between his thinned lips. He wasn't certain if he was shocked or pleased. His body's unexpected reaction to her put him in a sour mood.

His disposition darkened further as he assessed them. The two people he resented with every fiber of his being. The philanderer and his daughter. A swift scrutiny of her face sent molten flames of awareness spiraling through his veins. A fresh jolt of shock rocked his brain.

Why were memories he'd successfully deleted for years resurfacing? No. He wouldn't let them. It caused nothing but tortured, bitter feelings. It was best to damper the long-suppressed fury. A stab of regret pierced his chest. How could he ever let bygones be bygones? He clenched his teeth. He couldn't—

His billion-dollar world hadn't come without sacrifice. He'd struggled to build his business
empire, while men like Simon had simply shunned
him. Looked down their prestigious noses and closed
doors around him. The successful hotel magnate had
nearly ruined him when he destroyed his mother.
He'd worked extra hard to gain respect. He hadn't
forgotten. He swore he'd make them pay. He'd
sworn he'd flaunt his achievements in their faces.
He'd sworn to become more successful, wealthier,
and powerful. And he had. He now held that position.

This meeting, this day, wasn't happenstance.
It was years of strategic planning and calculated precision. Acquiring Watson Enterprises was only the
beginning. He'd set it up carefully, his intent to destroy them. He would own Simon's company and his
daughter lock, stock, and barrel. She was a pawn in
two callous, rich men's game. The Watson's would
rue the day they crossed paths with him.

He caught and held her speculative gaze.

He examined Angelica's frigid face. The
young girl he'd once known had certainly changed.
Gone were the long braids and gangly, tanned legs.
Gone were the metal braces that covered her teeth.
Gone was the innocence, the trust, and the idoliza-
tion she'd once shown him. But those deep, serious

blue eyes that once had enthralled him were the same.

His eyes lingered over her tall, sleek form. Her platinum-blond curls framed her heart-shaped face, and the sober black attire she wore conveyed strictly business. It wasn't her clothing that entranced him, but the endless miles of legs that tapered down to slender feet encased by red stilettos. The vibrant color was unexpected and briefly threw him off-guard. Without even trying she'd caused a reaction. Vibrant images set his blood roaring. His eyes flicked back to her face, and Julio forced himself to ignore the spiral of sexual tension that gripped him. He'd save that for a later day. What interested him was retribution. Adrenaline pumping, he felt grim satisfaction. He loathed Simon Watson. It would be a joy to make the old man squirm. Watson Enterprises was a meager reward. Simon would pay for his sins. Julio would exact his revenge. He vowed a long time ago that one day he would get vengeance.

A darker, sinister smile graced Julio's upper lip. The Watson's were making his premeditated planning easier. The prime opportunity fell right into his proverbial lap. He rolled back his broad shoulders and stood straighter, stepped forward and clasped her ice-cold hand between his.

He glanced down at the slender, pale fingers he held between his and quickly dropped it. The unexpected kick was inappropriate. He hadn't expected Angelica Watson to get under his skin ever again. It was purely physical, and yet it infuriated him.

"Isn't life full of unexpected surprises?" he inhaled an anticipatory breath. "Hello, Angelica. So, we meet again."

• • •

She gaped at him as he stepped aside and motioned for them to enter his inner-sanctum. What was he talking about? She didn't know this man. She knew of him and all his business accomplishments, but know him...not hardly.

Surely, meeting someone like him wouldn't have slipped her mind. "You must be mistaken," she shook her head. "We've never met."

"Trust me," he smiled, but it didn't reach his eyes. "We have."

His hypnotic eyes regarded her dispassionately. The rich, low timbre of Julio Suarez's voice slid over her skin like smooth, molten liquid sending shivers along her spine. She searched the far reaches of her mind trying to trigger a glimmer of recognition.

Nothing. Zilch.

She perused him further needing to make the connection. She hated being at a disadvantage. "Please, refresh my memory," she said. "I seldom forget a face."

Angelica looked around the sleek office surroundings searching for something, anything to spark her memory. The room was cold and impersonable like the man who dominated the space. Overstuffed chairs faced the polished chrome and glass desk. But nothing, no family photos, no mementos giving hints of the man behind the perfectly concealed face.

She shivered.

Julio stepped behind his desk and took a seat. He leaned back and steepled his fingers upon his chest and nodded leveling his gaze at her, a smile curving his condescending lips. "It was ions ago, huh Simon?" He said, turning to her father his penetrating blue eyes frosty and condemning.

The two men faced each other neither giving an inch. "Forget about the past, Suarez. I'm concerned about the present," Simon retorted, taking a chair before propping his foot on his knee.

"Believe me Simon, our past definitely affects today," Julio glared at his hated adversary.

"Is there something going on here that I

should know about?" Seating herself into the oppo-site chair she smoothed the hem of her skirt as Julio's eyes did a once over of her legs.

"Suarez and I go way back," Simon told Angel-ica.

"Yes, way back," Julio added.

"Why am I just now hearing about this?" she eyed both of them with pure irritation written upon her face.

"It's nothing to worry your pretty, little head about, Angel," Simon said. We're not here for histo-ry lessons but strictly business."

"Seriously, Simon. Don't you dare patronize me," she crossed her ankles then uncrossed them.

"Please," Julio interjected, "your family prob-lems don't interest me. Your family dynamics are shaky at best. I'm a busy man."

Her eyes deepened to a tumultuous blue while fighting his. These two men made her feel demoral-ized. The lesser of the three of them. Surprisingly, it hurt for no apparent reason. Simon was expected, but Suarez, he knew nothing about her or her fami-ly dynamics. What was going on here that she was missing?

"Right," she agreed, swallowing the lump created from her scattered emotions, "business. You know what we're here for Suarez, money, and lots of it."

Intense blue eyes, chipped with ice, regarded her dispassionately. His stoic expression revealed nothing. What lay behind those chips of blue was anyone's guess. "Yes, money. The age-old answer to solving everything," he laughed.

Their eyes collided, before she broke contact. Intense heat pricked her neck and face. He was daunting. She would give him that. Tension filled the room. She crossed her arms to calm her rapidly beating heart.

She couldn't help but drink him in. He was the most amazingly handsome man she'd ever seen. Up close and personal he was something else. She wasn't surprised, he hadn't become Argentina's illustrious playboy and billionaire financier, without looking magnificent.

Grrrrr…whatever she'd been expecting, imagined or not, he exceeded it. He was taller than average, six-three or six-four. The designer suit accentuated his broad shoulders and dark complexion. His five-o-clock shadow outlined his chiseled face. A sprinkle of silver peppered his dark, black hair giving him a quality of distinction. Without close inspection it was easily missed.

Her eyes were instantly drawn to the opened vee of his shirt. No tie. The minimal glimpse of skin sent her heart rate catapulting. He exuded a lethal combination of glamour, danger, and wealth. Yet, his attributes irritated her instead of excited her.

Angelica swiped a loose strand of hair back behind her ear. "That's it," she asked, "you think our plight is nothing but fun and games? It probably doesn't matter to you, but our company's future is very important to me."

"Wait," he said, then held up his hand. He picked up a folder and opened it. "Let's cut to the chase," he continued coolly. "I've studied your company's portfolio in great depth." Mockery filled his eyes. They remained intense and fathomless. "Watson Enterprises needs more than cash," he pressed forward. "It needs to be restructured from ground up. And, frankly, it's a huge endeavor. It would be wiser to dismantle and liquidate the assets."

"What are you saying?" Her voice lowered an octave as her temper leapt to life in her sluggish bloodstream. "You want to tear our company apart? A hostile takeover? What's the plan, sell off our hotels one a time?" Her tone became frostbitten.

"Don't take it personal," he injected, giving her a dangerous smile. "I've seen this too many times to count. Pouring cash into forlorn companies isn't unchartered territory. It just isn't lucrative. If they aren't profitable then yes, I will." His expres-

sion didn't falter. "Your business is extremely vulnerable right now," he continued. "The sharks are
circling ready to step in at minimal costs."

She knew he was right, but it didn't make it
any easier. In her mind he was the shark.

Julio stood and came around his highly polished desk. His eyes flicked over her in an intolera-
ble manner. "Listen," he stated, his South American
drawl slow and precise. "Your company's valuation
is plummeting. I can cash in your holdings in a couple of weeks without much risk."

"You want to buyout, then sell our company?"
she stated hotly.

"In this instance yes," he shot right back.
She tried to ignore the tangy, citrusy smell of his
cologne. The subtle nuances of his aftershave permeated her sense of smell. Mystifying and all male.
His magnetic pull was intensified as he towered over
her five-foot-eight-inch frame. She'd never felt so
small in her life.

Men like Suarez strong-armed the compe-
tition. Overshadowing them and burying them in
the muck and mire. Although she knew he'd come
from humble beginnings, he certainly didn't reflect
it now. He was a vicious multi-billion-dollar tycoon
who stomped out the weak without mercy or shame.
If her blue eyes held lightening, she'd have struck

him dead. The animosity crackled between them.
His arrogance and sharp perceptive eyes com-
batted hers. Her plummeting heartrate robbed
huge amounts of air. The curve of his lips and the
all-knowing keenness of his dark bedroom eyes com-
municated all she needed to know. He was ruthless
with zero compassion. Trouble with a capital T.
He leaned casually against his desk. His nonchalant
position added to her irritation. "Let me explain,"
he started again. "I'm sorry, but your business isn't
a viable option. A cash injection doesn't make sense.
I've crunched the numbers, and they fall short."

He swiped his fingers through his thick, obsidian hair while scanning their expressions.

Angelica inwardly cringed, but her facial facade held firm.

Julio's expression showed boredom. "I know
the truth is a bitter pill to swallow, but let me lay it
on the line. In the last five years your numbers have
been catastrophic. Your production is dismal, and
your employee wellness programs are poor. Your
financials are bleak. I reviewed your profit/loss and
cash flow statements, and they're failing. I'm sorry," he continued, "but lack in stating the obvious
there are red flags everywhere. Poor management
and nonexistent communications have drained your
company." He took great pleasure seeing the sim-

mering anger in her eyes. "You've made bad decisions, Angelica," he shrugged his shoulders his voice holding no sympathy.

Angelica felt Simon's tension, and her own stomach twirled. She knew the facts and figures but hearing them coming from Suarez didn't sit well. Simon's mottled cheeks and slated eyes intensified. She understood his anxiety. Hers matched his. She hadn't made these poor decisions, Simon had. But what did it matter now? More importantly, she knew if Suarez didn't invest into their company, they would be in financial ruin. They'd fallen into a sad abyss in the last few years. Everything would be gone. She couldn't allow it. Oh, God, her life had already been full of loss.

"Past grievances have nothing to do with this, Suarez," Simon piped in. "Surely you see the value of our business."

"That's what you call our past." Julio's patience ran thin as his voice dropped dangerously low. "A grievance. My grievance is with you," his eyes locked and held Simon's. The veiled threat hung ominously between them.

A bitter taste permeated her tongue.

Her face remained schooled in a neutral expression. "What's this grievance about?" She was tired of this wordplay with no answers.

The corner of Julio's mouth formed a sinister curve. "Ask, Simon. I'm sure he'll give you the watered-down version."

She was half tempted to scream at Suarez. He was purposely being vague. He knew his power. He knew his strength. But those eyes, disconcerting and bright, momentarily made her forget where she was and why. His sinful lips made her pulse kick-start.

Stiffening her shoulders, she blinked redirecting her thoughts, and faced the Latin business mogul. Training her large blue eyes on him. Intense awareness flickered in his. Awareness she wouldn't give any credence. But in these extreme circumstances she had to be extra confident and secure. Discipline and diplomacy were key to formulating a satisfactory agreement that would profit them all.

"Look, Suarez," she said, keeping her voice monotone. "You and Simon can hash out your differences somewhere else," she amped up her leadership abilities. "I don't care. Like I said before, I'm here to conduct business."

Still, his eyes, his profile jogged a recollection, a memory drifted into her subconsciousness. She knew him, but how?

She shook her head reclaiming her thoughts then continued. "We understand the hurdles involved with saving said business. I would like to obtain a satisfactory resolution today."

His jaw twitched. He seemed detached, not convinced. His eyes held hers as if telepathically giving her hints.

She pushed onward. "We still bring a lot to the table, and you know it. We aren't some substandard business deal." She took another breath and looked across at him. "Our carefully planned business trajectory hasn't been completely unsuccessful. You know this," she added, her focus precise. "We've got hotels all over the world."

"There's no denying your past history," one dark brow arched.

His perpetual blue orbs drilled hers. Two turbulent seas fighting for dominance.

A power struggle at its best. A battle of physically heightened willpower.

Who would win?

"Suarez," his name suited him. It rolled off her tongue sounding breathless, not resentful like she intended. She flicked her lashes, "Then what's the problem?"

His eyes inadvertently shifted back to Simon.

Simon squirmed in his chair.

Angelica watched the interplay between the two and frowned. Her eyes blurred momentarily from the increased throb of her earlier headache.

Julio resembled a stormy rain cloud. Dark and mysterious. His furrowed eyebrows knitted in consternation and curiosity. He was a technological giant; a genius, according to some. It was public knowledge that he'd waltzed through his studies from an ivy league school gaining his MBA early. He'd dominated his peers, which gained him an envied but disdained title.

Her eyes held his as her tongue darted out to lick her dry lips. A nervous habit she tried very hard to prevent.

He followed her tongue.

The sheer magnitude of his stare sent bright, red heat flooding her cheeks. She wouldn't be human if she didn't feel the undercurrents swirling between them. Was she strong enough to withstand his heat? And there was that nagging sensation of recollection again. She studied his face hoping to pinpoint it.

"Listen, Suarez," she hesitated, struggling for words.

The tension mounted. An underlying current whipped through the room. Suddenly, nothing was visible but the dangerous man standing before her. She lost focus. Almost.

"There's no problem, Angelica, except now the fate of Watson Enterprises relies solely on me," he said, his dry tone divulging very little.

Simon stood suddenly, a belligerent look upon his face. "Don't make this personal, Suarez."

Julio cast his look onto Simon. "It became personal a long time ago, Watson."

Simon's cheeks reddened. "What do you want, Suarez?"

"You already know the answer," Julio threw back.

"It isn't the bottom line you're interested in," Simon shook his fist. "It's payback."

"Yes," Julio snarled. "For all your miserable sins. You held my mother's future in your dirty hands and you crushed her. Crushed her!" he reiterated. "Were we so beneath you? Were we? Now, I could buy you a hundred times over," he inhaled a steady breath. "No respecting man in my position would stop now that I have you flat on your face. Me having controlling interest in Watson Enterprises leaves the two of you at a huge disadvantage. If you want to play dirty, go ahead, I'll tear your company apart bit by bit." His eyes narrowed into cold slivers. "I'll make sure your creditability in this industry is buried forever."

The two combatants glared at each other, hatred filling their eyes.

Angelica's heart kicked into double time. Her fist clenched tighter while she gritted her teeth. This was insane. It caused a cold sweat to break out on her skin. Her fingernails imprinted half-moons into her palm. How could she trust him? His icy expression caused too many reservations. She was good at reading people, but this was unthinkable.

"Stop it!" Angelica jumped up. "Both of you," she snapped, placing herself between them, throwing her hands against both of their chests. If she didn't intervene, Julio was going to deck Simon onto his pompous backside.

Chapter 2

Angelica was furious at them both. "You two better tell me what's going on. And I mean now!" Julio stepped back his chest heaving. "You tell me," his gaze snapped to her face, condemnation written all over it. "You know exactly what's going on." He combed his fingers through his hair, his eyes blazing.

"Simon destroyed my mother and nearly destroyed me. You were part of it. You used me. Isn't that what Watson taught you, Angelica?"

"Angel," Simon interrupted clasping her shoulder, spots of red dotting his cheeks.

"Shut up Simon!" they both snarled at him. Angelica stepped away from Simon's hand. Not in the mood for his nonsense. This business meeting had turned into something dark and sinister.

Julio pushed on. "Angel, indeed," he laughed without humor. "A more fitting name is she-devil."

She took a step forward hyperventilation pressing against her chest. She sucked in razor-sharp breaths seeking calmness to replace her seething fury. She itched to hit him but tightened her fist instead. "How dare you insult me," she inched her chin higher and met his gaze firmly. "You don't even know me," she said, slightly bewildered. He leaned in, flecks of steel filling his irises. "Don't you remember?" She could see the faint lines of crow's feet at the corners of his eyes. "Don't lie, querida. Who could forget you and me, the beach, and a lot of bittersweet memories?"

It felt as if someone sucker-punched her in the stomach. Her mouth dropped open before she quickly shut it. A roller-coaster ride of long-forgotten memories came crashing to the surface. "Oh...my... God! Mateo."

Her first big crush. Her first kiss. Her first heartbreak, and her first boy-girl disappointment. Time fell away back to the summer when she was sixteen, when each day had been all about seeing him, being with him on the beach. The boy whose name she had imprinted upon her hip.

"Yes, indeed. Mateo. Julio Mateo Suarez," he nodded, dark, bitter undertones dripping from his cruel lips. "The introvert boy from the wrong side of town. The one your father thought money could annihilate."

And that was when she realized she'd been pulled into a trap. In that moment she wanted, more than anything, to turn and flee.

But she couldn't. There were so many factors

playing against her. She pressed her lips together.
She needed him. She needed this company. She
needed her job. Angelica speared a hand through her
hair. He had no idea what a mess this made things...
but what did it matter? The company's reputation
was in tatters. Her emotions were frayed. How had
things come to this? Desperation.

    The years had changed him. At eighteen he'd
been handsome, but now, he was simply drop-dead
gorgeous. Good years. She'd give him that. How
problematic that the boy, now man, still had the
power to make her pulse race. Her first love, her
nemesis, had dogged her memory for years, leaving
nothing but disappointments. And now, he had the
upper hand, leaving little room for any exceptions.
Recognition had only recently returned and already
her body longed for that brief cosmic connection of
their past. The euphoric tingling of the anticipation
and physical attraction between two young people's
budding romance. But it hadn't been real. None of
it. He hadn't been right for her, never was. There
had been hidden and underlying circumstances. He'd
used her, broke her tender heart, and cast her aside
without looking back. Stop Angel, she preached to
herself. Her limited romantic relationships were a
mine field of disastrous mistakes.

    Angelica did a quick turnabout giving her back
to him. "What's he talking about, Simon?" Her rag-

ing headache nearing a full-blown migraine.

"Rubbish," Simon countered. "Absolute rubbish."

Julio returned to his chair and clamped his
hands onto the glass edge of the desk. "Tell her Simon, tell her," he snapped. "Explain how you slept
with my mother, then cast her aside like garbage."
Angelica could sense his fury was nearing explosion.

"Then used your daughter to tame and silence
the radical teenage son. Watson Enterprises is nothing in exchange for the damage you've done."

Simon's fury matched Julio's.

If looks could kill they'd all be dead.

Heated anger blossomed upon Angelica's face.
"This meeting was nothing but a chance to orches-
trate your premeditated hatred," she flung at him.
"Simon did no such thing. You're insane!"

"No, not insane, but be that as it may," Julio
continued, "your company's future lies in my hands."
He didn't owe the Watson's anything, and he was
unapologetic for that. He picked up a sheath of papers intimidation chiseled on his face. "Read these
papers," he said, shoving them toward her. "I've
scheduled an emergency meeting with the board of
directors. We'll meet this week. Remember, I owe
you nothing. In fact, if I was wise, I'd cut my losses
and walk away. I suggest you convince me, Angelica, to keep you on in some capacity."

The documents burned her fingertips. The papers crinkled in her fists.

"What did you do, Suarez? How did you manage this?" Simon lashed out at the Argentinian's frozen face. "Our shareholders would never agree to this."

His gaze snapped back to Simon's. "Your shareholders were tired of your blundering mistakes, Watson. It took very little convincing for them to pull up stakes," Julio stated evenly. "Their loyalty tilted out of your favor a long time ago. I'm majority stockholder. They sold their stakes to me."

"Don't turn your personal vendetta into a business deal," Watson's flat eyes gleamed with malicious intent. "I thought you were smarter than that. Camila was a grown woman, Suarez, she was responsible for her own mistakes," Simon spouted off.

"Don't let my mother's name ever, ever cross your lips again." Hatred and betrayal remained implanted upon Julio's face.

Diamond-like shards flashed within Angelica's eyes. He was being a complete and utter bastard. She could stop this takeover. She would stop this. She'd been born into this, the hotel business. She'd dealt with CEO's and billionaires worldwide, so why was Julio Suarez intimidating her? Her voice sounded calm and professional---although she was far from it.

She tilted her stubborn chin higher. She met his ice-cold gaze firmly. "Give me some time. I'll buy the shares back. Let me put together the necessary financing, and we'll walk out of here and never look back. This colorful lie you're poisoned by has nothing to do with our company. Please, let me repurchase our stock, Suarez, and retain ownership."

His laugh was bitter. "You're fooling yourself, Ms. Watson. You're on the brink of collapse, and I'm your only lifeline. It's a done deal. It matters very little to me."

Fiery sparks lit the back of her eyes. She took a step toward him, puddles of pink infusing her cheeks. "I will not under any circumstances agree to this."

He shrugged his broad shoulders. "Doesn't matter, Angelica, the fact is I already own Watson Enterprises. You're a smart woman. I have nothing to lose, you, on the other hand, have everything. Your holdings cost more in upkeep than any profit they'll generate. I'd be more worried about keeping your job than trying to buy your company back." The boy Mateo was long gone, replaced by the heart-less Suarez. His look was intense without an ounce of warmth in it. "My, how you've changed Suarez. I can't believe I ever liked you," she willed her look to not sway from his. "It's funny that you have the audacity to point fingers when it's all about facts and figures. You're a snake," she shook her head. "How does it feel looking at people's faces when you go in for the kill?"

A malicious snicker cleared his lips. "That's business."

Angelica stepped back putting more space between them. Her eyes grew flat, the deep, sapphire pools filled with regret. "That's a shame you're heartless. I can see it's a waste of our time to ask you to reconsider."

Angelica frowned at the pure stubbornness upon his face. Julio had no intention of giving her the opportunity to buy back anything. Watson Enterprises was at his mercy. She was certain Julio would risk an absorption of financial loss before relinquishing ownership back to her again.

"Sorry, querida," his assessing eyes ran up and down her body. "There are perks to this acquisition, and I'm not ready to give them up."

"No, no, and no...this is madness, Suarez. Nothing you do or say will convince me to stand for this." The spark of awareness caused Angelica to bite her bottom lip. It was best not to let him see that he disturbed her at all, but he did. He was trying to unnerve her. Bait her. Get beneath her skin. She wasn't about to back down, ever.

"It might be madness, but it's the way it is. Accept it. The terms are outlined. I'm calling the shots." He wasn't smiling now, though, his eyes continued to gleam. "I worked damned hard to get where I am today. Take my advice, Angelica, show up for this meeting." His voice dropped even lower and more intense. "Don't show, it will end your chances."

He came around his desk crowding her personal space. Ignoring the way, he was standing too close, Angelica gingerly stepped back. She focused on the Buenos Aires skyline behind his desk. If he stepped any closer, she wouldn't be able to catch her breath. She had no choice but to look up into his damnably handsome face. He exemplified a wolf claiming his territory.

Her skin pricked with added annoyance. He was damn aggravating, but sexy as hell. Which made him even more aggravating.

A speculative light entered his eyes. It was fascinating how the deep blue pools enraptured her. The atmosphere had changed. Business had dissipated and sexual awareness had begun. She lifted her chin and crisscrossed her arms over her pounding chest. Angelica inhaled hard, and exhaled even harder, and wondered why she felt terribly disoriented. He may hold her future in his hands, but she didn't have to accept it.

Clearly the man had his attributes, but she

had her pride.

"You can't buy me!"

The corners of his mouth quirked up into that unbearably gorgeous smile, "I already did."

"Damn you, Suarez!" Angelica burst out hating how he made her skin sizzle with heat. "What do you want from us? You've already took our business, our livelihood, and our dignity."

His jaw grew taut with barely contained derision. "You'll see, querida," he promised, his eyelids shielding his sexy eyes. "All in good time."

Her spine snapped into perfect alignment.

"You'll regret this, Suarez. I promise you."

He didn't even try to retain his wolfish grin. "I look forward to it," he nodded, and threw back his head and laughed.

• • •

Julio looked down upon the bustling city nestled far below his high-rise offices. The heavy traffic was moving at a snail's pace. Hues of blue, orange, and pink sunrise filtered the horizon behind the city's skyscrapers. He had spent all night behind his glassed skyline, but got little sleep. Yesterday's meeting with the Watson's had kept replaying numerous times. He'd been working since daybreak. Early morning was his best time for introspection and reflection. Vigorous exercise and strongly brewed coffee kickstarted his day. He cupped the hot mug between his hands and inhaled the deep aroma. His torso was slick from sweat from his extensive workout. But right now, the heavy exercise and caffeine weren't giving him the satisfaction he needed. Angelica Watson was utmost on his mind. He needed a cold shower to cool his libido as visions of her kept filtering into his head.

He finally had the Watson's where he wanted them, but instead of peacefulness he felt discontent. He hadn't expected her to get under his skin. He couldn't shake the image of her slim, lithesome body from his subconsciousness. Physical awareness flowed through his veins. He took a sip from the cup; the hot liquid left a metallic taste on his lips. She resented him; he'd made sure of that.
He was a pro at what he did, yet, corporate raiders never got any validation. They weren't liked, it was as simple as that.

Julio hardened his heart to any sort of sentiment. It really didn't matter to him how she felt. His inability to forget her was simply an inconvenience. If not for them, his life could have turned out so differently. His mother would still be alive. He wouldn't feel so alone. Bitterness clutched at his abdomen.

He wiped his face with the towel wrapped

around his neck. His dark locks were damp against his forehead. Sweat burned his eyes, but he didn't care.

A commotion outside his doors drew his attention. He could hear his assistant's voice getting louder to warn him.

"You can't go in there, Ms. Watson," Maria said. "Mr. Suarez isn't expecting you."

Angelica burst through the doors uninvited. She swallowed hard, struggling to catch her breath. "I hope you're happy," she blurted out, her words faltering when she spotted his heavily perspired shirt plastered against his chest. "Simon had a heart attack after our meeting yesterday."

Julio pivoted on his heel his eyes pin-pointing the intruder.

"I'm so sorry, Mr. Suarez," Maria said, her face filled with distraught.

"No problem, Maria," he assured her. "I'll handle this."

Maria closed the door as she backed out of the office.

Julio examined Angelica's disheveled appearance, sporting the same clothes she'd worn yesterday, not shocked she'd crashed in. Icy distain dripped from her heated glare.

"How can you do this, Suarez? Destroy people! This is preposterous," her eyes sparked blue fire as she threw the vehement words at him. Her chest was heaving, and her heart was beating like a sledge-hammer pounding mercilessly against her chest. She would not lose this company her family had built, in spite of the blatant problems they were in. Watson Enterprises was past vulnerability, it was collapsing, she knew this. Her worst fears had become real.

Her nerves were frayed. She'd been up all night at the hospital. Her eyes burned from lack of sleep. The weight of the world had crashed upon her shoulders. She felt betrayed, not only by Julio, but by Simon. A betrayal of everything she'd worked for. She would die before she would admit defeat. This gave Suarez even more leverage. Her primary goal to succeed seemed unattainable.

"Not to be sadistic but your father has earned whatever he gets," he said. "Simon brought failure upon himself," he kept his gaze fixed on Angelica without exhibiting an ounce of compassion. No pity. Only satisfaction.

"You're a cruel, cruel man, Suarez. And to think I once thought..." she swallowed, taking a deep, shaky breath. Then another. She resented him. Hated him. His authority, his audacity. At that moment he made her feel so small.

So, trapped.

Vulnerable.

Angelica had learned a long time ago how to keep smiling under duress. Fake it. Although his heartless words were tearing her up inside.

"Thought what?" He stepped away from the windows and walked toward her before stopping.

"Spare me the melodrama," he said coolly.

"Why would I believe anything you say?"

Clouds of heat rose to her face. "Don't believe me. I don't care," she exhaled a frustrated breath. "Simon is what he is, but he's still my father." A single tear slipped from the corner of her eye. "I've already lost my mother, and I don't want to lose him too."

"Is he okay?" He questioned, proper concern failing to reach his eyes.

"He's fine. Perfectly fine," she managed to say, though it wasn't exactly true. Simon's health crisis had presented a whole new dilemma for her. "Not that it matters to you," she added. "He's recuperating."

He gave a low, brittle laugh. "It does matter. It certainly changes things."

His brash statement made her blood boil.

"This is no joke," she choked out. Her palms were sweaty and she simmered with anger. Something flickered in the depths of his cool, assessing eyes, something that made her pulse skip and her blood heat. "Who's joking, Angelica? I take business very seriously." His eyes glittered as they stared at each other. "It isn't my concern, Ms. Watson, why your business is where it's at, but why it's failing. Failure is not an option."

She stopped for a minute and frowned. "Simon isn't business, he's family. But then," her voice came out in a rasp, "you don't care about family."

"You have no idea," Julio's voice was a low growl.

"Then enlighten me," she said. "You claimed Simon killed your mother. That's nonsense. Your callousness killed something inside me, Suarez. You lied to me. I was a young foolish girl who thought she was falling for you, loved you," she whispered. She couldn't blame her present mixed emotions on teenage hormones. He threatened her very existence. Her sanity.

He leaned forward his signature, citrusy smell, combined with sweat, invaded her nostrils. "I never lied. Everything I've said is true. I never claimed to like you, never mind love you."

Her breath gushed from her lungs. She felt sucker-punched. It hurt. And for some bizarre reason her throat was slightly constricted. She swallowed and stepped back to regain some semblance of control. Her smile, when it appeared, was cynical, without feeling. Her pulse thudded and the blood thickened in her veins. She must regain balance.

She watched his brow rise with scrutiny.

She couldn't take her eyes off him.

He didn't trust her. She could see the wariness in his eyes.

She wanted to do something. She wanted to put him in his place. What was his place? In her bed? Horror thundered through her chest. What was she thinking? Had she lost her mind? Even her innermost thoughts were betraying her.

No matter how big a business deal, no matter how high the pressure, she always used proper business sense. But physical attraction and emotional distress left her senseless. This whole life changing scenario was nerve racking. Not to mention mortifying.

She was caught in a bleak tunnel. She could feel the pressure building inside her, increasingly mounting, demanding release.

She made herself take long deep breaths through her nose willing the panic to dissipate. The breathing exercise calmed her. This was wrong. The unfamiliar tingling in her stomach caused a lump in her throat. The last time she'd let a man into her life had been disastrous. She'd come out of that relationship with scars that hadn't mended. Her ex-Derek had used her. Professing love and commitment while he upscaled his business portfolio.

Simon had gone to great lengths, insinuating Derek into her life, to prove a point. A painful point. Angelica shivered. Her own father had prayed upon her vulnerability. Manipulating her. Trust had become a definitive word for her. Suarez was fully capable of lying to her to get what he wanted.

She wouldn't let Suarez do the same. He was rude, high-handed, and entirely too self-absorbed. The air vibrated with electrical currents of tension. She wasn't entirely sure what it was, but it most definitely couldn't be attraction. The snippets of desire flickering momentarily in his cool, assessing eyes, changed nothing.

This couldn't be construed as anything but business. She must, without preamble, nip her heightened sense of awareness when near him. She must remain guarded. Nothing could ever come of this lingering attraction. He had been off limits since their teenage fiasco.

A sexual no-no.

Business and sex didn't mix. Allowing Suarez to breach her personal barriers was emotional suicide.

She'd been down that road before.

He could take his perfect little body and tempt someone else. He might be a playboy billionaire and trap many women, but she was exempt. She had the absolute power to resist.

Thank goodness.

All of her pep-talks weren't curbing the strong
pounding of blood coursing through her veins or the
headiness of his presence. She'd been impervious by
men like him for so long she'd almost made a career
out of it. She knew what was being said about her.
The rumors surrounding her. She'd been the butt of
crude and rude jokes for so long she'd become immune to the snide remarks and comments. It still
hurt to think her peers thought so little of her authority and position.

And here she was, only a few hours with
Suarez, allowing her armor to crack. Losing her
equilibrium and years of cultured resistance. His
masculine appeal was deeply dangerous. She kept
internally reminding herself his sweaty sexiness was
an unwanted distraction. God help her, but she was
terrified. His brooding, intense look immobilized
her making it hard to concentrate. Her well-guarded
bodily responses were blatantly disobeying her.
She wanted to walk out and never look back. She
hated his smugness. His power to upset her.

"What do you want?" he asked coolly. His
voice not even bearing a hint of inflction or the inner turmoil she was feeling.

"I want my company back. I want to buy back
the stock."

He lifted his brow. "Do you?" he asked. "I do

have reservations about having a working relationship with you."

"What do you mean?" she asked, about to
cross her legs but thinking the better of it as her
fitted skirt slid upwards. She briskly pushed it back
down while his eyes followed the movement.

"Perhaps I find your close proximity a little
disturbing."

"Meaning?" she said briskly. A blush tinged
her cheeks. She knew exactly what he meant, but
she refused to expound on it.

"What did you expect?" he said, Julio rested
his elbows on the arms of his chair. "You're a beautiful woman Angelica, too beautiful. To say I'm immune would be a lie."

Angelica's eyes widened. A flash of sorrow
flitted across her face. In another lifetime she would
have been flattered. Ecstatic. Men like Julio Suarez
didn't mince words. He didn't need to. Women
flocked around him continuously allowing him the
opportunity to choose from lots of beautiful women.
Angelica didn't feel beautiful. She sported faint dark
shadows beneath her eyes from lack of proper sleep.
Her all-night vigil with Simon at the hospital were
certainly present. She worried too much. She'd
always been known to take the weight of the world
upon her shoulders. Losing her mom when she was

young forced her to grow up quickly. Simon had been well, Simon. Gone frequently and leaving her with nannies. She'd never wanted for anything, but she'd been lonely, so lonely.

She felt more offended than flattered. She didn't want him to want her. Desire her. It was difficult her family was in a crisis and Simon ill. It was bad enough they were being strongarmed by the Argentinian billionaire. And worse than all of that, her dang libido had reawakened.

"I'm sorry, Suarez, but if you think for one minute this arrangement is going to lead into something physical, you're wrong." She broke off, her voice choking. "I have no interest in sex," she snapped, "or in a relationship of any kind," she blurted out forcefully.

He lifted his lithe body from behind the desk and came around to confront her. Angelica pressed further back into the chair. His brilliant blue eyes glistened with purpose. She licked her upper lip suddenly not convinced of her staunch immunity as his overwhelming presence crowded her personal space. He clasped the arms of the chair and leaned forward. His nose nearly touched hers. She could feel the warmth of his breath. She tried to look away, but her eyes kept darting right back to him. A look of anguish mottled her face. For the first time she

noticed the scar that crossed his brow and the chips
of blue ice that circled his pupils. His sculpted lips
curled into a hint of a smile.

"Actually, querida, I think you're very interested in sex. I've had many years of experience," he
smiled, "and the body speaks its own language. And
yours, my sweet, little mamacita, is telling a totally
different story than your lips."

The man was confident, she'd give him that.
His eyes were hypnotic and mesmerizing. Oh, it
would be so easy to cave and let her inner inhibitions
slide. Business be damned. How do you resist temptation when it's staring you right in the face?

He lifted his hand from the chair and cupped
her cheek. His fingers were soft and gentle, and she
momentarily felt so weak. Cherished. Something
she hadn't felt for years. Maybe never. Simon loved
her, sure he did, but he'd groomed her for business,
socializing, and turning a profit. The bottom line.
His lips were closing in... inch by excruciating inch.
Her eyes fluttered closed. She could taste him, his
citrusy fragrance encompassing her. She licked her
quivering lips and waited and waited and then... he
was gone. Her eyes popped open and color flooded
her cheeks.

"And that, Ms. Watson, is how easy it would
be to kiss you," he stepped back, straightening his

arms.

Angelica swallowed and anger filled her. He played her! His presumptuous audacity. "How dare you?" she hissed. She sprung from the chair. Her head felt light, and her knees nearly buckled. They were all the same. Men. "Don't kid yourself, Suarez. It's not going to happen. Not now or ever. This is strictly business," she hissed, "Do you hear me? Business!"

She met his gaze full-on; her chest rising and falling in agitation.

Taking an incised breath, he strode forward again, his intent clear.

She threw up her hand. "Stop! Don't take another step." The words sounded sharp. Panic was lacing her tone. "I want clear boundaries, and you better not overstep them."

He didn't say anything. His pause crackling between them.

Julio laughed, his eyes glinting with merciless humor. "I could've kissed you," his mouth twitched. "Your body's response is undeniable."

Fury pooled in her belly and before she could stop it her hand flew at his cheek, but he blocked the blow. Blue fire filled his eyes. "Don't ever think you can hit me Angelica and get away with it," danger saturated his voice.

The threat of tears pooled in her eyes. "I

guess you know where we stand...," she refused
to let him see her cry. "Don't ever try to kiss me
again." Dipping her head, she pivoted on her heels,
and walked from the room with every last shred of
dignity she could find, his knowing laughter antago-
nizing every nerve ending she possessed.

• • •

Julio was in a very foul mood as he waited at
the exclusive downtown restaurant while dusk fell
over the city. The table faced a bank of windows,
which overlooked the inky, black water reflected
below. The wavering shadows of twinkling white
lights enhanced its choppy surface like a glittering
trail of diamonds. Earlier he'd gotten a full report
on Simon's medical distress and despite his instruc-
tions, Angelica Watson hadn't done anything he'd
said. She blatantly defied him, and he was angry.

What was wrong with him? Things were
progressing nicely. Simon's health condition had
opened another door allowing him to further his
plans. After meeting Angelica this morning he'd
made numerous calls cementing his negotiations
with the shareholders. They were on side. So why
wasn't he feeling satisfied?

Because he kept seeing Angelica, stubbornness creasing her brow. The subtle hint of dewy

moisture upon her luscious lips. The way her teeth imbedded them with nervousness. The wild hint of unwanted desire shimmering in the depths of her eyes as he'd closed in. She'd wanted him. He knew that. A vision of her naked, beneath him, sent a sharp stab of awareness shooting through him. He didn't know what to do with that. Kissing her would be unacceptable. A grave mistake.

What would happen if he'd done it anyway? He was only human. How much could a man take? The longer he waited the more his mind veered along a sensual path. Irritation escalated beneath the surface. His mind was downplaying his physical need of Angelica, but his body was having none of it. He impatiently tapped his fingers against the bright whiteness of the table cloth.

She was late.

He hated when people didn't show up on time. Time was a very important commodity to a busy man. His gaze kept darting to the entrance of the restaurant. Dio! Where was she?

"Mr. Suarez, do you need a drink?" The waiter asked him for a second time with a polite smile pasted on his lips. Then he took one look at his fuming face, as Julio waved him away, and promptly fled.

Julio's nostrils flared and his brow furrowed as he looked at his watch. Twenty minutes. Was she

going to be a no show? Irritation marred his temple.
He had zero tolerance for unpunctuality.

Then he saw her. The chandelier's lighting
emphasized the curls framing her enchanting face
sending a slight kick straight to his gut. Desire
streamed through his system at the sight of her.
Even irritated, he felt the punch. She was breath-
taking.

She thanked the usher as she spotted his location.

Their gazes clashed.

He got to his feet, murmuring a sour greeting
when she arrived, then pulled out a chair opposite of
him. She took the seat. Practiced restraint evaded
him as he lowered himself back into his chair. He
waited.

She appeared to be composed, but her fingers
clenched and unclenched the strap of her bag. He
watched the motion briefly before catching her eyes.
She smiled, disarming him.

He knew she was remembering their almost
consummated kiss.

"Suarez, I hope I didn't keep you waiting,"
she started, knowing dang well she had. She leaned
forward slightly while her tone was very businesslike
and brisk. "Thank you for meeting me. I felt that a
public place more suited my purpose."

Julio veiled his eyes. "And what purpose is

that?" he asked, waiting for her to continue. His expression implying nothing.

"The first being to back off," she said, her tone flat and clear. "This takeover doesn't make you a dictator," Angelica stalled, resting her eyes on him. "Quit texting me."

"You were late," he spoke harshly, ignoring her statement. "Don't ever keep me waiting again," he stated authoritatively.

She met his glare head on. "Did you hear what I said," she snapped. "Back off, and I was late for good reason."

"Why was that?" Julio enquired. "Checking on Simon?"

"Looking in on Simon is within my rights isn't it? I owe you no explanation," her blue eyes flashed. "I made it didn't I?"

"I abhor tardiness," he shot her a warning. "You must respect my authority."

"Then why are you here?" she asked politely, cynicism falling from her lips.

"Curiosity, I guess and," he continued, "technically speaking I'm the one holding all the risks. I call the shots."

"Really?" she answered.

"You have a problem with it?"

"Yes, but it was exactly what I expected," she added.

He cast her a caustic look. "Then what's this impromptu meeting all about?"

"We need to find a satisfactory solution," she added, "negotiate terms."

"Then get to the point, Ms. Watson. I have other, more important business, awaiting my attention."

His shortness angered her. He was a jerk. A damnable handsome jerk, but a jerk nonetheless. Angelica kept her face placid.

He drummed his fingers on the arm of the chair his impatience paramount.

"My business might not be important to you, but it is to me." She rallied back.

"You're no longer in charge, Angelica, I am." His sinew flexed as he leaned forward. He eyed his opponent with more than curiosity but sensuality. She was wearing a designer dress more suited for the bedroom than a business lunch. Bright blue in color it hugged her curves in all the right places leaving little to his imagination. Was she dressed to distract him? It was certainly doing the job. She wore a simple chain around her slender neck giving little to distract the eye. But there was something about the way she carried herself. Purpose, determination, and regal carriage set her out from the crowd. That distinguished air of sophistication money can't buy. But wealth did play a factor, wealth he now had, but wasn't born with. The frown on his face deepened, altering his expression. Wealth she'd always known. Money defined her. Old habits and old insecurities filled his gut. The hurt, resentment, and those fillings of rage that had consumed him as a young boy. The fact that his dad had died, crashing into a tree, and leaving him and his mother penniless.

He knew it wasn't right, but he wanted to hurt her like Simon had hurt his mother. Make her fill the abandonment that he'd felt. The desire to want something you can't have.

And she would---he would bring her to that. Why else, he surmised, would opportunity present itself?

He felt his senses stir, bubbling in his veins. Julio sat back, his gaze openly appreciative of her ethereal beauty, the softness of her blue eyes, the lushness of her lips, the sculpted edge of her high cheekbones, the brown tint of her skin, and the way her blond tresses captured the artificial light. An enchantress.

She was everything he wanted, but everything he despised. A lethal combination.

She sat poised on the edge of her seat. She put her bag down and clasped her hands in her lap. The waiter poured their water and left the menus. Julio's eyes remained focused on the swell of her breasts. Their pertness outlining her dress with perfect symmetry.

His mind felt temporarily cloudy as he tried to focus on her voice. He snapped back to attention. His mind had slipped into forbidden territory. The attentive waiter appeared again and took their order pouring each of them a glass of wine per Julio's request. She sat back once he disappeared, trying to formulate her jumbled thoughts. She took a sip of the wine and let its sweetness moisten her tongue. A tongue that felt too heavy to speak. But this was a conversation, a brutal conversation they must have. She had to play this out.

"Here's the deal, Suarez," she leaned forward putting on her bargaining face. "Simon has, huh, substantial monetary obligations that must be paid." She moved closer. "I want to continue to market our brand. We are a preeminent global hospitality company with a clear portfolio, and I want to keep it that way." She took a much-needed breath and continued. "Everyone is expecting a huge round of redundancies in the company. Stop it. I want our employees to feel secure in their positions. No cutbacks," she added. Her eyes darkened to a turbulent shade. "I know you're into mergers and acquisitions, but this isn't just a job it's my life," Angelica mumbled shakily, unable to drag her eyes away from his bold, bronze features. "I put a lot of pride into our business."

She struggled to take a deep breath now that she'd said what she came to say.

He stretched his long, powerful legs out beneath the table brushing hers in the process. An electrifying current zipped through her skin causing her to move back quickly.

One arched eyebrow lifted. "I'm not in the business of buying sentiment and guilty little secrets, Angel." His fabulous bone structure was formidable, the darkness of his lashes shadowed the brilliance of his eyes raking over her like slashing shards of ice.

The subtle use of Simon's pet name for her sent a plaintive cry of unease whirling through her. His aggressive jawline tightened. "I have lots of money, but you already know that. I can do or buy anything I want. But you can't put a price tag on some things," he smiled. "Things," he added, "that are impossible to get." His pessimistic eyes stayed heavily focused on her. "Things," he went on to say, "that warm a man's blood. Things that could cause a man to lose his head. Things, my sweet Angel, that are physical. And then there are things a kid from the wrong side of town can't achieve no matter how hard he tries. Things you don't understand."

His long, strong fingers wrapped around the wine glass. And for a flickering moment she saw hurt and derision fill his cold, speculative eyes.

"This merger is about making money, not losing it. And I'm not," his lips curved upward into a smile, "the big bad wolf. By the way," Julio paused and moved his hand to indicate the arrival of their food and waited for the waiter to refill their glasses and discreetly move away, "I've done my homework. Simon's gambling debts aren't my concern."

Angelica tried to keep her hands steady. She'd been in this business long enough to know Julio would've researched every dirty little secret. Plowed through every closet. And wouldn't be sorry for doing it. He'd know every dollar spent; business and personal.

But the part he might have missed is that she was tough. Smart. She'd done her homework. Suarez might be a financial wizard, genius, but he also took serious risks. Lived dangerously. She was on shaky ground here. She was technically only in charge until Julio decided otherwise. The board could very easily oust her out. Ultimately, whatever Julio wanted, the board would do.

The board's desertion was imminent. Convincing them Simon's heart issues hadn't affected her abilities. She was in a man's world. Her phone had been on fire. The board members were shaken by Simon's health scare. Every stripe she had was hard-earned.

"Why do this?" Her question cut through the

air like a knife. "You don't want our company, and you certainly don't want our debt," she stated, injecting her crisp, business-like tone back.

He paused in the middle of lowering his glass. His expression changed. Desire backlit his eyes. She recognized it but didn't accept it. And in that moment, this wasn't about business, it wasn't about money, it was about deliberate, unexpected simmering heat.

"Why am I doing this?" He took her glass and sat it down clasping her ice-cold fingers within the warmth of his. He raised her fingertips to his lips. "Because of this."

His lips brushing against her fingers sent spirals of fire racing through her veins. All of her pent-up frustrations were crashing to the forefront. Her skin sizzled with awareness. He was a powerful adversary. Angelica had falsely convinced herself she was immune to him. She was unsuccessful, one look from Julio Suarez and all her inhibitions flew away.

Mortified, she jerked her hand back. His priceless grin encased her letting her know her response hadn't gone unnoticed. He chuckled deep in his throat, a sound of triumph.

Her body trembled in spite of her resolve. This sparring match between rivals was giving her so many reservations. She was weaker than she thought. And extremely less in control than she thought. She was feeling needy, lonely, and in spite of the fire between them, a chill fell over her.

She picked up her bag and stood. All of her pep-talks and motivational speeches hadn't worked. She must put distance between them, and fast, before she made a fool of herself. Keep reminding yourself, she mentally told herself, that this man could jeopardize much more than her company.

"Did you think I would let you off the hook so easily, Angelica? Did you think I invest in crumbling businesses for charity? Apenas lo creo!" His voice was low and intense fueled by determination.

"This isn't for me," she said, "because I don't need you. Our company might need you, but I don't. I could walk out this door right now and never look back. Believe me, Suarez, I abhor men like you."

She looked him in the eye with what she hoped was a stern, matter-of-fact demeanor.

He casually leaned back lying his napkin aside.

"Go ahead," he waved his hand toward the door. "Walk out. But believe me when I say, Angelica, Watson Enterprises is played out. I suggest you do some preparations before you walk into my boardroom. My decisions are final. I could destroy your hospitality empire. With just one call," he pulled his phone from his pocket, "I could have your hotels sliced into pieces, sold, or sourced out to other

companies." His eyes held hers in place, frosty and determined. "It's within my rights to do so."
Hurt consumed her. Hurt that she was in this predicament. Hurt that what he said was true. Watson Enterprises needed Suarez; he didn't need them.

She wished she had the strength to do it, walk out and not give a damn. But so many people depended on her.

"What do you want from me?" Angelica fired back at him.

He held her gaze for so long she thought he wasn't going to answer, but then he nodded. "The deal breaker. You..."

"You broke that deal a long time ago, Julio. On a beach, leaving me standing all alone," she shook her head sorrowfully. "I'll meet with the board, I might be forced to work with you, but there is no me and you."

Chapter 3

Angelica dreaded this morning, Julio had called late last night after their awful meal, the board was ready to drill her. She had spent the night crunching numbers, printing projections, and preparing arguments to defend her actions. The outcome was dismal. Her eyes burned. She had to come with a plan, fast.

The congested traffic had made the drive tedious leaving her taut with nerves. Exiting the car, she pasted on her public persona and lifted her head taking in the towering high-rise. The headquarters of Suarez' luxury conglomerate, JMS International. The sleek modern glass and steel building seemed to mock her. The meeting was on the ground floor. Angelica felt all eyes on her as she entered Julio's domain.

She stiffened her spine and marched forward. Her heels clicked against the tile of the polished lobby.

Click, click, click.

In perfect rhythm with her heart.

She didn't look to the left or to the right, but

straight ahead.

She ignored the pretty receptionist who showed her the proper door.

It felt as if she was walking down the long green mile determining the verdict of her fate.

She was a key player in the drama playing out before her. She hadn't chosen this path, but she'd finish it.

The boardroom was full of suits, but there was only one she noticed, Julio, seated at the head of the mass of bodies looking cool and relaxed and every bit in control. His eyes landed on hers, and the exchange was tense like every encounter they'd endured so far.

"Please, take a seat Ms. Watson," he instructed. He pointed to the seat next to him at the head of the table. Pasting on her battle mask she moved forward.

Angelica sat in the chair offered to her. She crossed one slim leg over the other and leaned back, tapping her patent leather stiletto heel on the hard floor.

Expectant eyes waited.

Angelica clasped her hands in front of her.

This acquisition process made her look incompetent and vulnerable.

A legal pad with a Mont Blanc pen were placed in front of her. Picking up the ink pen she rubbed her thumb against its high-priced exterior. She trained her eyes on the group.

Julio cleared his throat. "Everyone is well aware that JMS International has acquired Watson Enterprises," he started. "Ms. Watson has joined us to ensure the smooth transition of the company's holdings."

Angelica leaned in. "No, let's get this straight," her eyes sharpened. "I don't want a smooth transition. I'm not happy about this take-over. I have plans to explore every avenue to pro-cure funding to secure our position. And in regard to company stock, I'm still a stockholder. I guarantee Watson Enterprises has complete confidence that we will bring the Watson brand back to new markets. Our luxury hotels have been a household name for a long time. Our customers are loyal and will con-tinue to be. I hope that JMS and Watson's can work together as long as it takes to negotiate terms," she added emphatically.

His eyes sliced to her. She'd angered him. Good.

"This takeover," he reiterated, "has many variables which need to be addressed. I have it on good authority that the figures laid out will take some manipulating to get in order. My accountants are working diligently to crunch the appropriate ap-proximations to turn this thing around."

"What variables?" she asked.

He forged on. "I've invested a huge capital sum in this endeavor, and I expect nothing but heavy returns."

"I agree to disagree," she smiled smoothly.

"To what?" he quizzed.

"To all of it," Angelica felt entitled to add.

"Watson Enterprises is in so much debt, the only thing that can possibly save it is to sell off some of the assets and invest the funds into more lucrative ventures."

"I don't give a damn about your huge capital," her eyes lit up with consternation. "You've negated all our terms. What you're doing is immoral."

"But legal," he said, folding his arms across his chest, "my team has gone over all the tangents, and it's the only solution."

"We talked about keeping stability within our company. Jobs, benefits, and company morale."

"My goal here is to help you, Angelica. Help yourself. And in doing so, I must make executive decisions that are sound."

"And you don't care who's toes you step on?" she uncrossed her legs and tilted her head to the side.

"Exactly," he stated. "Is there a problem?"

She arched her finely groomed brows. "Yes, there's a problem. What happened to morals? To honesty?" She placed her hands on the table and leaned forward. "What happened to protocol and business ethics?"

"What part of "I make the decisions" did you miss? My corporate policy was clearly outlined in the prospectus. I trust you read it?"

Suddenly the crowded room seemed empty. It became two combatants circling each other attempting to gain control.

She sucked in her breath, her heart thumped, and Julio felt a strange, answering jolt in his gut. She was beautiful. Exceptionally beautiful.

He checked himself for the directions of his thoughts. This wasn't the time or the place. He needed complete concentration. She was an enigma he wanted to crack. It was interesting how she made him feel. He hadn't been this intrigued by a woman for a long time. Maybe never. She wasn't afraid to thwart him at every turn. Go head-to-head with him. She possessed a lethal weapon...she could use his response against him.

"I read it. I'm not stupid, Suarez."

He moved his head, a lock of dark hair falling forward with the motion. "Then you're well aware this takeover is happening."

"The shareholders may have caved under pressure, but I'm not," she stated, looking around the room. "You have no power over me."

"Don't I?" he asked. "Watson Enterprises is in trouble, Angelica, you know that. Your profit margins are so deep in the red that the alarms have sounded." His eyes held an intensity that left her dangling precariously on the edge.

She was married to this business. Had been most of her life. She knew the nuances of its operations. She didn't need to be reminded of the failures. She pushed down her anger. She wouldn't give him the satisfaction. "I'm well aware of our circumstances. No need to remind me. But as CEO and co-owner I'm focused on the company and its best interests," she added. "Things have been grim, I agree."

He paused for a moment, his smile widening, void of any emotion, but just as devastating. His five-thousand-dollar designer suit gave him an additional edge. "The board of directors tend to agree with me. You and Simon have mismanaged things to this point. Simon's health issues have basically put him out of commission for the time being," he reiterated. "We need to bring things up to date, modernize, and cash flow the properties. Pull it from the grave."

How did she argue the truth? It was a pointless. She looked into his eyes, the gleam in them filled with something so dark and assessing that she felt it reach into the depths of her soul. And that was when she realized she was unimportant, powerless, in this game of corporate hierarchy and Suarez's personal vendetta. She would move forward, make informed decisions, and try to maintain her position. This was her life, her responsibility. She must keep her chin up and carry on.

"I'm not on board when it comes to making callous decisions." Swirls of dread encased her chest. She knew what he was saying made sense. She has been sinking for a while now. Hanging on desperately with the wild hope that she might perform a miracle. And here sat her miracle in the form of a billion-dollar-man with the mind of a financial wizard.

"There is nothing callous about smart business," he replied. "Trust me," he carried on, "I know the difference."

Angelica looked around the mildly interested faces. She'd nearly forgotten they had an audience; her focus being totally centered on Julio. "Do you?" she asked.

Julio's gaze examined her stern expression. "You need someone in charge who is objective and knows what they are doing. Someone," he added, "whose got their head in the game and isn't letting their emotions, instead of brains, make crucial decisions," he added, his eyes unrelenting. "Your fathers laid up. He poses no threat to me."

Sure, she'd admit, personal connections were playing a part in her decision making. Her grandfather had built this business from the ground up, and it was their family heritage. How could she let it all crumble to the ground? Let her family's business empire come to an unhappy end? How could she defend Simon? She had to stand firm and remain loyal to the company, her grandfather's legacy and mostly to herself and what she believed in.

It was sacrilege to let a stranger with no connections or affiliations to the family be placed in the driver's seat. A headstrong Latin dynamo who had no qualms about dissecting the very thing that kept her sanity.

Where was her business sense? She felt like she had the weight of the world upon her slender shoulders. Responsibilities she had no choice but to bear. Failure seemed imminent. She was fighting a losing battle. She'd been a master of deception. She'd bottled up her feelings for so long; she didn't know how to do anything else. Her dreams, her desires were nothing but a vague memory. A shadowy image pushed to the back recesses of her mind. Something she no longer let take root. The only thing that mattered now was validation. Business validation. Her only position was to take charge and find necessary solutions to get back into the black. She couldn't and wouldn't eliminate jobs. Her employees depended on her. She would not fail. It wasn't an option.

She narrowed her eyes. "I haven't been the figurehead of this company and not known what I'm doing. I have a degree in business, and I've got a head for numbers. There have been various factors that were out of my control. But I know," she kept steady eye contact, "I'm an asset. And," she concluded, "you'd do well to remember that."

"Bravo," he said. "Of course, that all sounds good in theory, but is it? As the principal investor I'm in the position to veto any and all decisions that don't further my plan."

She furrowed her brow. "Suarez?" A shadow moved over her face. "It seems to me you've no intention of abiding by my suggestions. How can we improve a company you've decided to tear apart it's infrastructure? It means something to me. It doesn't matter to you. You are in the business of ripping companies apart to reach the bottom line. And I, on the other hand, am in the business of traditions. Taking what's available and making it last."

"This is business, Angelica. You know that," he said, his blue pools steady and true. "Personal complications are another dynamic."

Julio looked at Angelica. Her eyes didn't stray from his. They didn't flicker or flinch. The curve of her neck with all that alabaster skin briefly fascinated him. She remained uptight, oozing loads of dignity and restraint. He'd give her that. She'd perfected the image she wanted the world to see. In public anyway. But in private would her image be so infallible? Would she show a warmth and affection beneath her stern exterior?

Her cool, blue eyes gave nothing away. Not even a hint of weakness. The light pink gloss outlining the fullness of her lips gave them an added shine. She played her part well. A stiff, upper class business woman dressed to perfection.

"Family is personal, Suarez." Her lips pursed, and her eyes dueled with his. "For instance, what's happening now has a lot to do with family. Your mother is dictating decisions. You go home at night to emptiness, don't you? No wife, no children, and I bet," she paused for effect, "not even a dog?"

He flinched. "Family is personal, and yes, retribution seems fair."

Hardness reflected in his assessing gaze. She'd hit a nerve. A nerve he didn't like to discuss with anyone, especially not a room full of suits. He waved his hand and ordered the group to leave the room. Amidst the scraping of chairs and shuffling of

feet they cleared the space. Then there were two.
"My family, or lack thereof, is none of your business," he hissed, when the room emptied. "I don't
need people or pets to make me happy, querida.
I've found the initiation of people in your life caus-
es nothing but problems. At least a dog is loyal and
doesn't expect anything in return."

"Do you have one?" she queried, intentionally
riling him.

"Have what?"

"A dog? A pet? Anything to comfort you at
night," her eyes deflected from his.

"No," he said. "But comfort at night, as you
so aptly put it, isn't a problem."

His knee brushed hers.

"What makes you tick, Suarez?" she questioned, inching her knee from his contact.

Color heightened his jawbones. She was asking things he wasn't willing to answer. His personal life wasn't up for discussion. He thought of his
mother. Her weakness. Her sorrow. He curled his
hands into fists, blinding hurt consuming him when
he thought of her. The frail broken woman she'd
become. She'd died in poverty and sadness. She had
never gotten a chance to make a difference. He had.
He was. He helped children across the globe. Children liked him. The child he'd been. The child
who'd been sad and lonely. And wanting something

he couldn't have and he couldn't get. No amount of money or success could give him that. His foundation implemented programs and scholarships for numerous children and teens.

He swallowed making his Adam's apple look more pronounced. He should've turned down the opportunity to buy shares in their failing business. Would the taste of poetic justice be worth the problems that confronted him? Angelica Watson. A woman with a fortress built around her heart. A woman with sex appeal oozing from her very pores. But trying so hard to contain that natural energy. A woman who was tampering with things that he was unwilling to give.

What was her motive?

"What truly matters to you?" Angelica asked.

"Nothing," he finally said, "except making money. Lots of money."

She frowned. "Why? You've already mastered the art of making money. You told me yourself you can buy anything you want. And I know this to be true. What else is there?" she asked.

"I need neither the money or the company," he stopped and considered. "You're right I conquered it a long time ago. It's the challenge. The buzz. The kick."

"You get a thrill from another's suffering,"

she probed.

"You're misunderstanding my motives," he explained. "I like to take what is broken and put it in someone's hands who will improve its efficiency. Giving it a fresh innovative boost. Reinventing it so to speak."

"You're right," she agreed. "I thought this arrangement was simply a bail out. A loan to get us back on our feet. But you," she eyed him wearily, "turned it into using your voting rights to undertake novel measures in controlling Watson Enterprises. That was never your intent, was it? You bought controlling interest behind our back."

Julio compressed his wide, sensual lips registering her heightened agitation. "You knew going into this JMS International profited from corporate raids."

"I had hoped this time was different," she injected softly. "I wanted us to be on the same playing field."

His eyes glinted. "Why would you think or expect that? I've been clear from the beginning. The expectations were clearly outlined."

"And I told you at our dinner meeting what I wanted and expected," her professionalism was beginning to collapse. Instead, irritability was taking precedence.

He leaned back, the light catching the fleck of silver in his hair. "So, you did. Did you honestly think I would give it consideration? Approaching business idealistically isn't practical. I'm proceeding as planned and once you realize this is the only option moving forward, I trust you'll get on board."

"Do I have a choice?"

"Not anymore," he answered.

Her throat convulsed. She swallowed the lump lodging there. She stood, her knees wobbly and weak. "It would appear I no longer have any authority. What am I now," she asked, "an executive without a title?"

Very little touched him except business, power, and profit margins, but business took precedence. "I'm afraid you are a victim of circumstance, Angelica. Outdated policies, your dad's highhandedness with money, and poor business practices have landed you here." He shrugged his shoulders. "Like it or not, I'm your savior, and you're stuck with me." The thought of the Argentinian magnate saving her didn't have any sort of appeal Actually, it scared her. A boy who'd risen from the streets to become one of the most powerful men in the business was daunting to say the least. Admittedly or not, women were still the minority on the corporate ladder. She'd acquired the title rightfully by family legacy.

She wasn't a pushover. Never would be.

"All I'm concerned about is Watson Enterprises."

He leaned further back in the chair. Extending his legs out in front of him he crossed his ankles bringing her eyes to his black patent leather loafers that cost more than most people's house payment.

"This is doable, Angel." His dark lashes briefly shaded the intensity of his eyes. "Relax. Your lifestyle is still intact."

Angelica bit the inside of her lip. "Is that what you think I care about? My lifestyle," she said, her voice level.

"Isn't it?" he quipped. "I've rubbed elbows with many upper echelons of society and that's exactly what they care about."

"Then apparently you haven't done your homework, Suarez," she tilted her chin up, exposing the long, elegant length of her neck. "I refuse to be categorized with the bluebloods of society. My blood runs red," she snapped.

He stood matching her for height. She stepped back, but he countered her. He cupped her chin between his thumb and forefinger. The electrical current zipped straight to his groin. His response to her was uncanny. He didn't want it. However, he was a realist, and there was no sense in denying

the obvious. And no matter how hard she fought it;
he knew she felt it too. A tinge of pink colored her
cheeks, her lips slightly trembled before her lashes
sheltered the spark of awareness that invaded her
eyes. Her chest tightened when he refused to release
his hold.

"Oh, I've done my homework, Angelica,"
he said, dropping his hand and releasing her chin.
"You've convinced the world you are immune and
erected a shield. But," he leaned in refusing to let
her ignore him. His vibrant eyes intent on hers.
"You need me," his breath mingled with hers, "for
more than my money."

She took a step away from him, her heart
thundering in her ears. "You really are a cocky bastard!" she injected sharply. "Other women might
succumb to your," she paused searching for the right
word, "less than admirable charms, but I'm not other women. I will never...never fall into your bed,"
Angelica slammed at him.

"Never is a long time," Julio countered. "Every woman has her price."

A red haze blurred her vision. The audacity
of the man. He thought she could be bartered for a
price. Except, if she admitted it to herself, he did
tempt her. Excessively. Being near Julio Suarez
made her feel things she'd thought she buried a long

time ago. Things she never let herself dwell on anymore. Feelings, if allowed, tormented and haunted
her memories. But when she was alone, in the priva-
cy of her bed, she let herself dream about things lost
a long time ago. Dreams of finding a man to share
her life with and to love her unconditionally. Foolish
dreams.

"Not everyone and everything has a price,
Suarez. Don't ever insult me by suggesting I do."
Julio flashed her a grin, teeth bright against his dark
skin. "It isn't an insult to state the obvious. The
spark's there, mi amor, why deny it?" His all-knowing eyes flickered to her lips.

Having him so close, she suddenly felt jittery
and a bit nervous. It made her stomach tighten with
knots. She was allocating it to her constant stress.
For the past several months she hadn't had time to
think about anything else except finding solutions to
their financial crisis.

She'd given up so much to save the company.
Long hours and sleepless nights had taken a toll on
her physically and emotionally. It only hit harder
when she walked into her office each morning faced
with adversities. She had come to the conclusion she
couldn't fix this mess. And then Simon had implemented his master plan of bringing Suarez on board.
Now look what she had to deal with. A man who was

making her feel things that had been better off dead. Julio was different now. He made her feel differently too. He was edgier, colder, less unforgiving than when they'd been young. Maturity had given him the edge to unnerve her. To get inside her head? His appeal had broken through some of her guarded barriers. She'd worked so long and hard to form an emotional detachment. Emotional immunity.

But his dark eyes intent on her, and his body language humming with energy had shattered her resolve. Somewhere in her guarded, locked away heart was a romantic, with romantic notions. But to him her feelings didn't matter. His agenda was completely opposite of hers.

Her mother had believed in love. But she had been nothing more than a business deal. A merger. A marriage of convenience. Angelica had watched the life be snuffed out of her mother long before the cancer had taken her body. Her father had withheld all the important ingredients for a healthy marriage. Love and affection.

Angelica wasn't going to ever fall into that trap. She'd seen her mother imprisoned by marriage to a rich, callous man. If she withheld her heart and kept her head, she'd never follow in her mother's footsteps.

"I think you've lost your mind,' she said. "The spark you so aptly described is a figment of your imagination. I feel nothing toward you," she said crisply. "Not like, or hatred, and certainly not desire." Guilt rode her shoulders. All made up lies to convince herself. Because the last thing Angelica wanted was for history to repeat itself and for her to fall deeply in love with the worst kind of enemy. A rich and powerful man holding the burnished key to her business and her shattered memories. She wished she could hurt him the way he'd hurt her. She turned and laid her hand on his forearm, her professionally manicured pink nails, neon-bright, against the darkness of his jacket. Proving she could touch him without so much as a flicker. "And never assume you know what I'm feeling because you don't," she added for effect.

He clasped her slender hand and with absolute deliberation raised it to his lips. And with the same deliberation he kissed her innermost wrist. He felt her pulse jump and leap from beneath her skin. You would've thought he'd kissed her lips.

He relinquished her hand, letting his gaze linger on her. He heard her slight intake of breath and that was enough for him. He saw the speed in which she wiped her hand against her hip.

Pure satisfaction filled him.

He re-caught and held her wrist. He tilted his head, looking down at her. His lips parted, while his thumb rubbed her skin. Angelica shivered, horrified how easily he could crash her defenses.   "Don't un-derestimate the power I possess, Angelica."

His words mocked her.

Angelica couldn't speak. Her shoulders sagged, and her eyes stung. She watched him; her breath tight in her chest. She swallowed, paralyzed into place. Her mouth felt like cotton, bone-dry and parched. A part of her wanted him no matter the consequences, but the hurt and angry side wanted to scream at him.

His hand fell over hers before she could pull away, he reeled her in with little resistance. She gasped as her body made contact with his.   Then Ju-lio, aka Mateo, was kissing her. Her long ago fanta-sy became a reality. The pressure of his lips coaxing hers into submission. She felt his manhood harden against her. She did not resist when his fingers en-twined into her hair tilting her head back making her mouth more accessible. Everything inside Angelica short-circuited. Alarms sounded as his mouth made her hormones dance.

He was temptation personified.

The kiss deepened and her insides burst into flame.

She wanted him. Oh, how she wanted him.

She felt deprived when he pulled away. With-out saying a word, Julio Suarez still had the last laugh. For a second or two she clung to him not trusting her legs. Trembling with sensations she was afraid to name.

"You want me, mi amor," his breath was hot against her cheek. "Your company isn't the only thing I have within my grasp." Ice dripped from his mouth, dousing the liquid warmth coursing through her veins.

She chewed her bottom lip, anger simmering inside.

"You're wrong, Suarez," she pulled back. "I don't want you. I want my company."

He laughed and gave her a sardonic look. "Convince me, Angelica," his jawbone clenched. "Under the right conditions I might consider it."

Was he suggesting what she thought he was suggesting? Business for pleasure.

"Have you lost your mind?" she threw back.

"On the contrary. Now that I've tasted your lips, I want more." Every line in his face was set in a hard angle. "Once challenged, I always win."

She tried to hold onto every last shred of composure she had. In the background, people were milling about. They were laughing and talking, continuing on with their daily lives. The world was still turning. But her life wasn't so simple. Her world had just become much, much more complicated.

Chapter 4

Angelica was quite relieved to put some distance between her and Suarez. The man was infuriating and way over confident. Her lips still tingled from his kiss. She fell right into his web.

Annoyance marred her brow. The slow burn of his eyes and mastery of his lips had caused her to lose sight of her goals. Goals that didn't include distractive pleasures. Goals that did include company retrieval. Goals that would keep Watson Enterprises intact.

She had a business to save.

And Julio Suarez was not going to win. She'd see to that.

Simon had been in this business for a long time. He had fallen short on so many levels, but he had numerous connections. Although he'd been associated with the terms arrogant, egotistical and narcissistic he still had a lot of influence with people in high places. Not too many years ago he'd been at the top of the corporate ladder.

She knew what she needed to do.

She picked up her phone and dialed Simon.

"Simon," she paused when he answered. "How are you? The doctor said things are stable," she added.

"Are you feeling better?"

"I'm fine," he assured her.

"Good," she said, getting to the point. "Who do you know on the appropriations committee?"

He cleared his throat. "Why do you ask?"

"You know Suarez has plans to build that gigantic new resort. Word is he's got a lot riding on it," Angelica said. "There's been behind the scenes rumors of skepticism and grumbling. I don't know why I didn't think of this sooner."

"What are you getting at?" Simon quizzed.

"What if his permits got tied up in red tape," she jumped in, going straight to the heart of the matter. "Without the proper authorization his investments would be unavailable. Watson stock, and it's problems, would become a big burden," she paused.

"Don't you think?"

Simon cleared his voice again. "Gomez, my golfing buddy. He has a lot of pull when it comes to these things."

Angelica's mouth twisted as her plan took shape. "Contact him. Bury those permits."

"We went to him, Angel." Simon sighed.

"For a cash injection, not a takeover." After what Suarez had done, she felt absolutely no reservations. "You could've died, Simon. You had a heart attack. I know he'll eventually get around it, but it'll buy me some time to find a lender willing to work with us to buy back what's rightfully ours."

"He's a very astute businessman, Angel, he can easily destroy us completely. He's already got it in for us," he added.

"I know that," she stated. "But it's a risk I'm willing to take."

"He is a self-righteous SOB and a risk-taker," Simon laughed. "It won't hurt my feelings if you put him in his place. But be careful, Angel. He will be furious."

She blew out a mouthful of air. "I need all the ammunition I can get. This is our only chance to even remotely retain Watson Enterprises. It's under-handed, I know, but he deserves all he gets."

"I'll see what I can find out," Simon finished as they ended the call.

Angelica laid down her cellphone and felt a surge of pure satisfaction.

An image of Suarez, on the beach, his eyes full of sadness and hurt, sprang to mind. The feel of his lips as they coaxed hers. She shuddered, goose-bumps raising the fine hair on her forearms. She was having a moment of feminine weakness. She shoved down all hints of regret. No. Like he'd told her. It's strictly business.

• • •

The cold jets of water splashed over Julio's body. Thank goodness for the fully appointed bedroom and ensuite bathroom attached to his office. His body was overly sensitized and all man. After several excruciating minutes his body was finally starting to settle down. He was mad at his own flesh. His weakness.

And Angelica Watson was the cause of it.

When he held her in his arms, he'd nearly shattered? Madre de Dios, in that moment he was ready to give her anything. He'd strongly considered forsaking his vow to destroy her and Simon if she'd agree to come to his bed. It was a fool's mission. But she was so vibrant and alive, and her body's involuntary response to him was unbelievable.

He wanted to ruin her, yet possess her. She'd always been out of his reach. All his old insecurities came crashing in. It made absolutely no sense, these unwanted feelings. He prided himself on sound judgement and decisions.

But as soon as his body had molded against hers, common sense had deserted him, and male reaction had overpowered him. Physical attraction

and reaction were powerful aphrodisiacs.
His reaction to her was astonishingly bad behavior.
And he hated it.

Julio prided himself for being in control and his control was slipping.

Stepping from the shower he toweled himself dry and got dressed. He'd almost forgotten her ulterior motive. Her company. She was really getting under his skin.

Stupid, stupid, stupid...he berated himself. One more minute, one more kiss, and he'd been tossing her on this very bed, sheathed deep inside her. A man had to be careful, in the throes of passion, it was easy to lose basically all logical thinking. He might have promised her anything. And everything he'd accomplished would've been lost. Years of careful planning tossed in the wind.

Back in his office he made no move to check his phone messages or scan his computer. If he'd looked down at the string of messages it would've infuriated him.

His mind was far from business, but still on the woman he'd kissed. She'd asked if it bothered him to go in for the kill. Well, the answer was yes. A piece of him died every time he tore apart someone's business or livelihood. It was grim satisfaction at best. He'd learned to harden his heart to any emotional attachment.

However, the hurt caused by the Watson's had fes-
tered and grown. It'd torn him up for so many years,
he didn't know how to act differently. Seeing her
hurt and misery was simply part of the game. It became personal the night his mother died. He should
terminate her and leave it at that.

Something clutched at his insides. Pity or sorrow? He wasn't ready to label it. All he knew was
seeing Angelica again had set off a chain reaction.
He could not or would not allow her to get inside his
head. He had to carry out his master plan.

He simply had to move forward with his revenge. Angelica would end up in his bed. Their
physical attraction was all too real. Her responsive
kiss was all the proof he needed. Getting her into his
bed would be physically satisfying for both of them.
It was the perfect answer. The old adage... keep your
enemies close... was good business strategy. Seeing
the Watson's cowering at his feet was a pretty picture indeed.

Julio looked down at the string of messages on
his phone screen. His attorney, Andre Martinez. He
read the words while curses rolled from his lips.
Julio, you're not going to like this. The Watson's
somehow got your permits buried in appropriations.
The bureaucratic hassle could tie up your new build
for quite some time. How do you want to proceed?
Fury filled his face as he tapped on Martinez' name.

How the hell did they manage that? He'd put an end to this ploy...

. . .

The pounding on her door came as no surprise. News spread fast in the business community.

Angelica could feel his anger vibrating through the barrier of the wood. "Angelica, I know you're in there. Open this door."

Nervous tension filled her throat. Knots filled her stomach. The gloves were off and now she had to face the repercussions.

"Angelica," his voice lowered, more threatening. "I said open...this...door."

She knew she couldn't keep him barricaded outside for much longer. He'd probably break the door down. She pasted on a fierce, ruthless smile and turned the knob and pulled inward.

His shoulder gained access first before the rest of his body. She jumped back to avoid a collision. The door hit the wall with a bang. He was mad. Wrathful fury was written all over his face.

He grasped her shoulders and shook her for added measure. "Maldito seas! What have you done? This is unforgivable."

She stood straighter, taller, not giving an inch as he removed his hands. "Now you know how I feel."

"I should've never let my guard down. You Watson's are dirty dealers," he hissed. "You'll stop at nothing to get what you want."

She fisted her hands at her side to keep them from shaking. She needed to stand firm. Keep focused. "Never challenge me Suarez. I'll always win."

She threw his previous words right back at him. Swearing, his face turned a darker shade. He looked murderous. Something kicked low in his gut when he looked at her. The physical jolt was unwelcome and unwanted. Her hair was pulled up into a messy bun on top of her head. Several curls had escaped the black rubber band. Diamond studs graced her earlobes capturing the reflective light. Her jeans weren't tight but still outlined her long, slender legs. But her jutting breasts, pressed against the front of her worn T-shirt, sent an instant erection to his groin. That really made his blood roar. How could he want this woman he literally hated?

"You won't get away with this," Julio's words snapped like a whip. "I know people too."

"Do you?" she had the audacity to ask. "No matter who you know, the ball has been set in motion, and it'll take a while to stop it."

He stepped closer, breaching the dead space, and her body quickly responded. His magnetic eyes sizzled with awakened fire as he sensed her immediate reaction. "Oh, I'll stop it," he assured her, ignoring the tip of her tongue wetting her lips. "I'm privy to your ploy, Angelica, and it's not going to work. I'll do everything within my power to make sure you never regain your precious company. So, all this trouble was a waste of both of our damn time."

"You can't stop me, Suarez," she promised. "I'll find the money. I don't care what I need to do."

His eyes landed on her, sinful and cold. Her breath caught in her throat. For a moment she forgot who he was, transfixed by his physical beauty. "What would you do?" he said, moving toward her with lethal intent. "What price are you willing to pay?"

His thumb and forefinger caught and held her chin. "This," he leaned in his breath warming her face, his mouth only a fraction from touching her lips. "We can barter a kiss for a kiss, a touch for a touch, I have no problem with that exchange if I can taste you," Julio pressed onward. "I really want you," he said, just to see the shock enter the deep recesses of her irises.

Her pupils dilated, but she didn't look away. Her reddened cheeks a telltale sign of the frustration his nearness was causing. "If you think kissing me is a game changer. You're wrong." She captured and held his condemning glare. "You can kiss me all you want Suarez, but it doesn't matter." Her self-satisfied smirk made his jaw clench. "Your paperwork is buried waist deep in red tape. I made sure of that. You only want to get under my skin," she added.

She stood straighter unknowingly biting her lip. His intent was clear and Angelica's bloodstream vibrated with anticipation. She wanted to feel the pressure of his lips upon hers. Her mouth swiftly parted, without taking her eyes off him.

Her obstinate nature was a stimulating challenge. He placed his finger beneath her chin, tilting her head back. She closed her eyes before it happened.

His lips crushed hers coaxing, welding and prying until she parted them and allowed him access. Everywhere his tongue stroked ignited a flame of heat.

She made a choked sound deep in her throat. This was unfair. This spell he put on her. As her body became softer, sweeter his kiss deepened causing her to forget all the past, the future, nothing but the present. This moment when her mouth was melting beneath his plundering lips.

He'd breached her barriers. Something she wasn't ready to concede. She could handle his anger. His resentment. Her heart fluttered then skipped a beat. But this...this sweetness of his thrusting tongue, toying with hers, making her want a whole lot more. As soon as his hands found and massaged her backside, she felt like such a hypocrite.

Everything inside her went into high alert. Alarms sounded everywhere crashing her senses with a loud, disturbing noise.

She jerked back. Gasping a lung full of blessed air. She looked away from him not able to meet his satisfied grin. "You had no right, Suarez, to kiss me." Her chest rose up and down with agitation. A side effect of her guilt.

"Si, bella," he said, not ashamed at all that he'd made her lose sight of the circumstances. "I want, need, to do more than kiss you," he arched his dark brow. "I think you know that."

"I won't admit any such thing," she gave him an annoyed sideways glance. "Using male persuasion is unbelievably unfair."

"Imagine it, querida. Imagine how it would feel." His eyes toyed with hers. "Haven't you thought about being in my bed throughout the years?"

"It never crossed my mind," she uttered the falsehood without batting an eye. "Business and pleasure never mix. I've been down that road before and I'm sure you have to. Anyway, is that why you're here? To try and sway me by hot kisses?"

"Is that what you think? That my kisses are hot?" He smiled that dark, sexy smile, causing her stomach to somersault.

"Stop it," she closed her eyes briefly. "You're trying to twist everything I say."

"Don't misunderstand me, Angelica." He stepped forward closing the gap between them.

"Bedding a woman doesn't mean that I'll make concessions or change my mind. You're still the enemy. I still don't like you and I want to make you pay, capisce."

The hair on the back of her neck rose. A furious haze entered her eyes. His triumphant grin added to her aggravation. "Keep that in mind, Suarez, when your huge investment is tied up indefinitely. Remember, I told you so. And "bedding me" as you so aptly put it isn't on the table. I'd rather die than sleep with you."

He recognized that she needed to mask the veil of desire surrounding them. She fiddled with the loose tendril brushing against her cheek. He desperately wanted to release the band and let them all fall down the slender arch of her back. He wanted to pull her into his arms again, but decided against it. "You and I are more alike than you think, Angelica. We'll stop at nothing, by using whatever means, to get what we want."

"You're wrong," she shook her head. "We're nothing alike," mixed emotions were stamped upon her face.

"What's the difference, bella? Explain it to

me." He leaned in again, but she stepped away. He smiled, knowing his proximity had reopened physical responsiveness. "Denial won't change it, Angelica. You're lying to yourself and to me," he paused, gliding the back of his hand against the softness of her cheek. His eyelids dropped leaving only slits. "Have you forgotten that my name is branded upon your hip?"

She clenched her fists, skin tingling from the brush of his touch. "That was a mistake. A young girl's stupid rebellion." She sucked the corner of her lip between her teeth. "You're a selfish, cruel man, Suarez. I'll never be fooled by you again." She inhaled a fresh gulp of air. "Simon and I came to you in earnest for help, but instead we got nothing but disillusionment. You are a bully," she lashed out. "I don't trust or believe anything you say."

His jaw muscle twitched, anger suffusing his face. In that brief moment something changed. She swore he flinched. She almost felt sorry for him. But then she hardened her heart. He hadn't earned her sympathy. He deserved it. He was ruthless. He didn't care who he hurt in the process.

"I'm not sorry for what I did."

He crowded her space when the back of her legs collided against the sofa preventing her escape. His laugh was bitter. His eyes sparked resentment.

"And I won't be sorry when I reciprocate."

Her throat ached. She knew he meant it. Maybe she'd taken on more than she could handle. Julio Suarez was a worthy adversary.

He thrust a hand through his devilishly dark hair. "It would've been wise, Angelica, if you and Simon hadn't tried this preposterous delay tactic." His eyes speared her with bitter scorn.

"What choice did we have? You wouldn't listen to reason," she continued. "We're not responsible for your misery, Suarez."

Something flicked within his eyes so briefly that she couldn't decipher it. A cold, proud shell plastered his countenance. Angelica had the sudden urge to comfort him. Hug him. Fix this wedge they'd both created.

What was she thinking?

Had her brain short-circuited?

His mobile device dinging interrupted her rebellious thoughts. The sound reverberated in the quietness surrounding them. He reached in his jacket pocket and pulled it out, frowning at the screen. The sexual tension was immediately erased. Darkness shrouded his eyes. His jaw muscle clenched tightly as he read the text. A vein popped out in his neck and his mouth tightened, forming a hard, stern line. Whatever the message, he didn't like it. Not one bit. He reached out, then changed his mind. "Damn you, Angelica," he spit out. He moved mere inches, turned as if to say something more, then slammed the door in her face.

Chapter 5

Julio shouldn't have over reacted and tested his ability on the playing field he'd created. Produce problems that shouldn't exist. He'd underestimated her. He should've known better. His heart jumped a beat and he suddenly went ice cold. His behavior had become unorthodox since Angelica. And he didn't like his rash decisions.

He'd been on the phone doing damage control ever since he'd left her place. He'd finally got the green light he needed on the permits. His fast talking had repaired the mess created by the Watson's.

He sighed and leaned forward and looked out the bank of windows from his high-rise penthouse. Only the best was to be expected in the world he now lived. It provided exceptional panoramic views of the Buenos Aires skyline. Twinkling lights flickered in the night sky forming a firefly effect. The city's rush hour traffic was noisy in its bustling fast-paced chaos far below him.

The Suarez de Mayo building in the Palermo District was created from his own design.

He swirled the drink in his hand, the ice clinking against the glass.

His intent eyes focused on the stillness of the dark horizon. He breathed in slow and deep, striving to focus.

He thought this takeover was going to be easy. By exhibiting control over Simon Watson, it was going to give him the grim taste of liberation he had sought for so long.

This business motto was too personal. Phase One: Take control. Phase Two: Manipulate. Phase Three: Revenge. Phase Four: Sweet taste of Success.

If you had the looks, power, and the money, people were susceptible to you if used effectively. If he played his cards right, it opened a lot of doors. With people, there was always vulnerability and weakness; you just had to find it and cash in.

His entrepreneurship had flourished and prospered beyond anything he could've imagined. Throughout the years, he'd established, built, and sold companies. His wealth had expounded world wide. His success was no joke. He was passionate about his job. He had built a global empire.

But Angelica Watson had broadsided him. The gangly teenage girl he'd rejected all those years ago was now an incredible woman that invaded his thoughts frequently, but this little fiasco wasn't setting too well. He would straighten it out but it was causing him an added headache.

Thousands of times through the years.

It had kept him awake at night when he'd least expected it.

Her forbidden memory.

She'd never known who he was and now a slight grain of guilt filled him.

He'd come to her under false pretenses. White lies. Simple half-truths. All the lies he had told her, and all the unkept promises nagged at his subconsciousness.

Air filled his nostrils. The rapid staccato of his beating heart pounded against his chest. Suddenly, reaping the rewards of his success didn't seem so grim.

He reflected on the young teenage boy he had been. His mind lapsed back to that time. That fateful summer so many years ago. Rewinding the film projector on the memories he oftentimes tried to forget. His mother alive; vibrant and smiling even though the toils of work and stress had taken their toll.

. . .

He knew it was against the rules to bother her at
work. Not to interrupt. So, he was often alone. The
endless stretch of beach outside the Watson home
is where he ended up so many times. And that is
where he first saw her. The skinny, little blond prin-
cess, running on the sand.

He'd been kicking the football ball around
waiting for the time when his mother could go home.
The sparse little hovel they lived in.

The untouchable heiress in the bikini had
wanted to capture his attention. And he'd let her.
The introverted boy with a huge chip on his shoulder. She didn't know him or that his mother was in
her house. An employee her dad was using for fringe
benefits. He cringed when his young eighteen-year-
old mind went there. But he was old enough to understand the mechanics of sex.

"Hey," she smiled and waved.

He didn't wave back but stood with his foot on
the ball.

He cast her his lop-sided grin; his dark brown
curls unruly against his brow. His deep bronze skin
caused her heart to beat a little faster. And at sixteen Angelica had her first major boy crush.

"You from around here," she asked. "I've never seen you before. I'm Angel," she said, and stuck
out her hand.

His velvet blue eyes locked on her, but he ignored her hand. She dropped it back to her side and bit her bottom lip.

"Something like that," he answered back. "I'm Mateo."

Having him so close made her stomach tighten. She felt all jittery and silly. She'd never seen such a handsome boy. He was to die for. Wait until she told her friends. His moodiness only intrigued her that much more.

"Oh," she let her voice trail off, not sure what to say next.

"What about you," he asked suddenly. "You live around here?" He already knew the answer, but he wasn't going to let her know that.

She smiled prettily. She pointed, "Yeah, right up the beach."

His stomach flip-flopped. Her smile was causing him to slip. He hated everything that was Simon Watson including his self-indulgent, spoiled daughter.

"Yeah, I know," he admitted, "I've seen you before."

Angelica's eyes widened. Her heart skipped a beat. "You have?" She shifted from one foot to the other suddenly conscious of all the tanned skin she had exposed. She was too young, at sixteen, to draw attention to herself, but suddenly what he thought counted. He made her feel different, this boy she didn't even know.

They kicked the ball around, swam, then sat on the beach and talked the rest of the afternoon. About school, friends, what they liked to do. They somehow liked the same music, movies, and even some of the same foods. He gushed about his mother. She told him how hers had died and how she missed her terribly.

They met on the beach every day for a month. No one bothered to enquire about her whereabouts. Her dad was too busy with his life to worry about her. Angelica was positive she was in love. Not caring that a girl her age was too young. She would've run away with the quiet boy who'd stolen her heart. She wasn't naïve enough not to know she was caught in a fairytale comprised of her vivid imagination. Julio aka Mateo had become a prominent force in her life. A young girl with all the material things money could buy except happiness. And he'd brought her happiness. Loads of it. His presence had bridged the gap of the endless hours of loneliness she felt. They both craved the same thing. Companionship. Angelica had never known he'd given her his deceased father's name and not his own. She never knew his mother was the flavor of the month for her dad. She just knew this boy made her feel things that her tender heart had never imagined. She never doubted him.

Yes, they were worlds apart. Opposite sides of the spectrum. Julio regaled her of life in the slums. The misery that surrounded him each day. She had commiserated with him, but she couldn't truly understand.

"Don't you have lots of other boys you can hang out with," he asked. "Boys from the right side of town?"

"No," she answered seriously. She stuck her pert, little nose up stubbornly. "And, anyway, I don't want to hang out with anyone else." She batted her doe-shaped eyes at him. "I really don't care what people think," she said. "I want to be with you."

He wanted to believe her, but his battered ego still resisted. He didn't want to like her, but he did. The more time they spent together, he found himself telling her things he'd never disclose to anyone else. His deep secrets. His desires. His dreams.

She told him about the family business.

"What about your dad," he asked. "Don't you want to follow the family footprint?"

"Never," she stated adamantly. "I saw what it did to my parents. I might get thrust into the business but I won't make the same mistakes as my parents. My marriage terms will be a lot different."

Sadness filled her eyes. "The misery my mom suffered when she thought no one was watching."

"I'll be there someday," he promised. "I'll have enough money that my mom will never suffer again."

Even at her tender age she knew he would succeed and find great success. Angelica could feel it deep in her soul. The tortured boy who held her young, impressionable heart, would climb all those insurmountable mountains they had talked about.

That night they'd cuddled on the beach. Forgetting time. Forgetting problems. Only depending on each other. Night had slipped to dawn and then to morning.

Angelica had panicked. She'd never been late. Never stayed out all night.

Simon was furious. Surprisingly he'd known about her gallivanting on the beach with an unsuitable boy, Julio Suarez, Camila's son. "He wants nothing but sex," he'd yelled. "How convenient for a poor boy to get my daughter pregnant!"

Angelica had been mortified. Her innocent mind had never considered sex. Her dad was disgusting. She tried to explain, but Simon wouldn't listen. He forbade her to ever see the boy again.

She cried for two days. The non-emotional kid with the broken heart.

She yelled at her dad until she was depleted and told him he couldn't keep her from him. She branded the boy she loved on her hip permanently. Two hearts tattooed with the names Mateo & Angelica Forever. And with no regard for the consequences Angelica had disobeyed her dad and went back to him.

"Let's run away," she pleaded. "Take me where I can never be found again."

She showed him the hearts and it made him angry. He made a rude sound. "Are you crazy?"

Hurt and confused she grabbed his hand and held on for dear life. At that moment, only his approval mattered. "Please," she whispered, "I know this is crazy, but I just can't stand the thought of never seeing you again. If my dad finds me here, I'll be grounded for life."

Julio withdrew his hand and pushed her away. He had to end this. He'd never intended it to go so far. To grow into the blossoming relationship that could never exist. Her boy toy. A temporary distraction to amuse the spoiled rich kid. A summer fling. And he wasn't going to be anyone's fling. His madre was making up for that. It shamed him that they were pawns in the Watson game.

"Go back to your beach castle," he said, his eyes darkening with ominous dismay. "I don't want to ever see you again."

Waves of hurt consumed her, making her ears ring, and her throat constrict. She couldn't believe what she was hearing. "What are you saying? Please," she said, covering her ears with her hands. "Please take me with you?"

He clasped her forearms and held her at arm's length. A muscle flexed in his cheek. "I'm sorry. This was a mistake. Simon was right. I was trying to take advantage of your stupid innocence. Now I'm bored."

His words were like burning metal branding her skin. Harsh bitterness filled his voice. He was a stranger again and all their time together quickly disappeared.

She had to do something. Make him understand. Because his anger was tearing her insides apart.

Standing on her tiptoes she pressed her lips to his. The impact was electrifying. Her first kiss. The moment she'd longed for. The moment she couldn't resist.

At first, he was unresponsive and then his tongue entered her lips. Burned against her sensitive skin. The shock sent her into a tailspin. She closed her eyes and let the sensation wash over her. And then her tongue dueled with his. Her inexperienced body melted against his. Burning her up. And for a breathless moment the world ceased to exist. Everything was perfect.

But it ended all too quickly. He lifted his head and Spanish curses flew from his lips. And from the look in his eyes, she knew they were finished.

The pain swirling in her eyes was mirrored in his. The raw emotion of a lost love tore her to pieces.

He just looked at her for a moment his chest rising and falling with short, labored breaths. "We can't," bending over he his hand drew a line in the sand. "We're from two different worlds," he said. "You on one side, me on the other. Someday when you're older you'll understand. Nothing but a grain of sand on a great big beach."

He paused, about to say something, and then shook his head thinking better of it. He turned and swiftly walked away. She wanted to hurl. She felt like she was going to die. Her heart cavity held a hurt beyond comprehension.

Julio wanted to turn back. He truly did. His young heart ached for something he knew he shouldn't want. He wanted to hold her quivering body and promise her everything was going to be okay. He wanted to mend the broken thread between them, but the girl he dreamed of didn't exist.

Chapter 6

Julio Suarez was kissing her. Kissing her soundly. His kisses were igniting every need inside her. His damn eyes. Sinful grin. His toned, sleek, delicious body enraptured her.

His intensity immobilized her brain cells.

His muscles flexed beneath her fingertips.

All thought processes temporarily froze.

His jaw muscle clenched with resistance.

He pulled back. She licked her lips. The taste of desire slammed her taste buds. The taste of him on her lips. She was on fire. Her veins pulsated with the rush of heightened levels of hormonal awareness. Sweat tickled her brow.

He could sense it.

Her primal radar was skyrocketing. She clamped her fists imbedding her fingernails into the delicate skin. She thought she'd been prepared to face him, but nothing had prepared her for this.

The instantaneous attraction.

God, he was forbidden fruit. The kind of fruit that once you tasted the sinful nectar, there was no turning back.

It was too powerful.

Dynamic.

Her gladiator. Renowned for his ability to make women swoon. Her erotic fantasies packaged into one male specimen. It wasn't hard for Julio to be the delight of all women.

He was full on male.

The deliciousness of his kiss flowed deep into her desire ridden body. She suddenly felt deprived of his touch. She wanted more. Lots more.

His languorous gaze lowered to her slightly swollen lips.

"What is it you want, querida? You see what you do to me." He took her hand and placed it over his pounding heart. "I want to kiss you, Angel. Really kiss you."

"I know," she whispered. "I want you to. I mean," she added, "to really kiss me."

"If I carry you through that door," he pointed to the bedroom. He eyed her intently. "I want no regrets. Do you promise," he asked sternly, "there will be no regrets?"

"Yes," her softly spoken admission prompted him. He tangled his fingers in her hair and dragged her gaze to his. In that moment he had absolute power over her. She could not resist. He slid his hand behind her neck and dragged her mouth to his.

It was no tender kiss. It held all the pent-up desire they'd been skirting around from the moment their eyes had met.

His mouth slanted over hers, and his tongue tangled against hers, stroking, caressing, his taste sending hunger barreling straight to her nether regions. He deepened the kiss; pressing his hand along her waistband until he felt her flesh. His touch against her over-heated skin sent shivers careening up her spine. He splayed his fingers over her rib cage until he cradled the undercarriage of her super sensitized breast.

She moaned. He tore his mouth away and then leaned his forehead against hers. Their labored and ragged breathing making them both out of breath.

Any doubt she had evaporated. And all they'd done was kiss. Sensation overwhelmed all logic. "Take me to bed," she demanded, her raspy voice sounding like phone sex.

"You're sure?" he quizzed, giving her one last chance.

She moaned, totally overcome. "Take me to the damn bed!"

"Bossy much?"

He chuckled and then crushed her lips. A deep, demanding, stroke of tongue on tongue.

He lifted her into his arms pressing her high, full breasts against his chest. She tossed her head back letting his mouth devour her neck. He marched with her through the room placing her on the massive bed.

The masculine bed was positioned against the far wall. Across from it, its gas flames flickering luminous blue in the darkness, a floor to ceiling modern fireplace graced the wall. The flickering artificial flames cast shadows upon Julio's face, taut with need, and consumed with a passion so deep it made his blue eyes seem almost black.

The bed dipped as he came down with her in a tangled heap, his mouth, hands, tongue working all sorts of magic on her heated flesh. Her shy, hidden fears vanished beneath the onslaught of his lips. This red-hot fire that made her forget everything but him.

"What do you want, mi amor?" he whispered against the erratic pulse crashing in her neck.

"You," she said firmly, her hand sliding down the expanse of his back. "I want you."

The sexual awareness nearly exploded between them.

Angelica knew it the instant they entered the room. She trembled; he'd made her want him more than she had ever wanted anything.

"Suarez," she groaned, running feathery strokes along his jaw. Feeling the hot, sexy stubble that shadowed his chin. The sandpaper rough whiskers felt coarse against her over sensitized skin. Suddenly she was super-hot and bothered. She didn't know where he stopped and she began.

He found the hem of her skirt shoving the fabric up and over her hip. His lips continued to perform an erotic little number on her burning pert erect nipples that craved him.

He raised up, and her closed eyes popped open feeling bereft without him.

He smiled, and his eyes lit up. His finger traced the outline of the intertwined heart tattoo that was permanently affixed to her hip. "What's this?" He knew what that tattoo meant, he wanted to hear her say it. Say that he meant so much to her when they'd been young.

She sought out his eyes and smiled impishly. "A memory from a long time ago,' she shook her head. "A boy who shattered my heart and then left me alone. Why, Julio? Why did you do that to me? I thought what we had was special."

Julio's heart lurched, and his pleasure was intense. "I must've meant something, querida, since my name is on your hip?" A cloudy vision of the spirited, blond-headed girl branding him with her innocent kiss, twisted his gut. That girl no longer existed. Was it his fault? Had he defined the woman she'd become?

"It was an impulsive, teenage reaction," she promised him. "It's a reminder," she looked down at the imprint, "of how boys, then men, leave you craving more than they're willing to give."

He pulled back, a frown marring his darkened face. He hadn't liked what she said.

But come hell or highwater she wasn't going to let him stop because she wanted, no she needed this. Splaying her hands against his chest her nimble fingers found the buttons and undid them exposing his well-honed chest. She raised up and licked the man nipples that she'd revealed within.

An anguished cry escaped him. He pulled up her chin and kissed her like he'd been starved of her kiss. She feasted on the nectar of his lips.

She wasn't a virgin, but she'd never experienced a seduction like this. It was catastrophically intense.

He stripped out of his clothes. Aptly displaying all his naked glory. His bronzed flesh rippled and the tightly honed muscles sculpted into washboard abs. She couldn't take her eyes off him. They remained glued to the wide expanse of his chest. She mustn't lower her gaze a fraction of an inch because she knew he was fully aroused.

When he came back to her, he removed her clothes with practiced ease. The red sheets caressed her skin. Every inch on fire for him.

He propped up on his elbows and examined her every square inch. "You're beautiful," he breathed, his desirous eyes deeply intense.

And she felt beautiful, wanted, and needed. It was a heady experience.

"So are you," she smiled shyly. "I mean irresistible. Let's take this to the end."

Her heart had been numb way too long.

And then he kissed her. On and on and on and then some more until she squirmed with unquenchable need. He splayed his hands upon her waist. His lips found her burgeoning full breasts and he drew one nipple into his mouth sucking until she thought she would die from it. Her nails clawed his back and her legs wrapped around his waist. He fiddled with the bedside drawer until he found protection. She watched as he rolled it onto his manhood.

And then he entered her. He touched her womb in a cataclysmic collision. Fireworks exploded. The kaleidoscope of vibrant colors flashed behind her closed eyelids.

"Julio," she screamed, as unimaginable orgasmic convulsions shattered throughout her body.

Then he reached his own deafening crescendo.

Angelica whimpered in his mouth as he carried her home with his mind drugging kiss.

He rolled to the side pulling her with him. Sheens of sweat dampened their clinging bodies. She sighed softly stretching until her limbs intertwined with his. The silence was palpable as their breathing returned to normal.

She suffered no regrets. The sex was definitely enjoyable. She'd never felt so sublime in all her life. He was one hell of a lover but then she'd known that. Nothing had prepared her for the enormity of all this. This one night of spontaneity took them to a whole new playing field. A whole new level.

A new normal.

How would she face him now? Frustration gnawed at her stomach. It was different when two people had sex. Actions and reactions became strained. She hated the worrying game that would begin.

As soon as the fantastical euphoria wore off, Julio would withdraw and make excuses for himself. Derek had done it every time. And their sexual encounters had never compared to this.

Angelica held her breath when he began to move. Here we go, she sighed. She might as well get the upper hand on him.

She lifted her head, then shifted, pulling away from him. The separation cooled her skin. She hated the stilted small talk in the aftermath. She hated the waiting game. She hated rejection. She couldn't handle all the emotional garbage after just having great sex. She didn't have all the answers, but she didn't want to wait around to hear his. Who cares that he'd made her gloriously float onto cloud nine?

A state of perfection.

His brows furrowed together creating a divot between them.

"Well, that was nice," she said, pulling the sheet around her flesh. Her intentional withdrawal was pretty evident.

He lifted his arms behind his head and leaned back into them. Dark color slashed across his cheekbones changing his expression to shards of ice. He didn't like what she was saying. He trained his eyes on her. His schooled face gave away nothing. "That was nice," he repeated what she said. "Ay, caray!" he swore sullenly.

She was having a hard time remaining neutral with all his exposed nudity.

"I didn't come here intending to have sex with you, but I'm glad I did," she cast him a blank stare.

"Oh, dios!" he injected. He stood, his spine ramrod straight, coiled tension radiating from him.

He strode across the room, his tight buttocks blatantly on display.

Renewed tingles of desire gripped her midsection spiraling down to the area between her thighs. He returned with a towel slung low around his hips.

She knew she had annoyed him.

"It was more than damn nice, Angelica," he flattened his lips. "We had sex and it was great. You need to tell it like it is. I don't like comparisons."

She sat up straight pulling the sheet with her. "Who said I did," she attempted humor, but it fell on deaf ears.

His ominous mood sent her to silence. "I don't care about your past sexual history. I take making love seriously, and I'm as monogamous as you get."

But his look sent a shiver speeding down her spine. "But," she waited.

"It was sex, great sex, and I liked it," he retorted. His words, when spoken next held all the cold, calculated hints she knew were coming next. "In today's world," she popped back, "sex doesn't mean anything. People do it all the time and walk away. No commitments, no attachments, nothing but friends with benefits."

"Friend is a subjective word," he was quick to add. "We understand each other perfectly. I'm not interested in a relationship. Don't get me wrong... I'm interested in more sex." Julio studied her with glittering, wicked eyes. "I've never wanted a family or a wife, too much invested interest. I'm the last man in the world you would want to go and get any emotional interest in."

"Exactly," she tossed back. "It doesn't matter who initiated this. It just happened. Nobody's been changed because of it."

"Right," he agreed. "I never let sex get in the way of business. Our little romp between the sheets doesn't give you any sort of edge."

"That being said," she snapped back, looking at him. The man was so infuriating. "It certain- ly doesn't give you any sort of edge. Or bragging rights."

He was furious and it showed. "I don't kiss and tell, Angelica."

"Don't you," she countered back. "I've seen your picture plastered all over magazines with vari- ous conquests."

"Not because I chose to put them there." He raked his fingers through his hair. "And don't be- lieve all you have heard and read. Newspapers and magazines are the masters of invention."

"Hmmm...isn't there some truth to every sto- ry."

"Why does it matter anyway?" He caught and held her gaze as he sat on the edge of the bed, his towel slipping several vicarious degrees.

"It doesn't," she agreed.

They'd reached an impasse.

She rolled to the edge of the bed taking the sheet with her. The sheer force of the physical release they'd shared was more than she could wrap her mind around right now.

Making her escape was imminent.

The huskiness of his male scent and the closeness of his body was killing her resolve. Another romp between the sheets was quickly becoming forefront in her thoughts. Now that she'd tasted him, she wanted more. Natural instinct.

Her body was still humming from the after effects of his pleasure.

"Where are you going?" he asked, his eyes like magnets beneath his intent glance.

She looked back over her shoulder as she gathered her scattered clothes from off the floor. "I'm getting dressed."

"Why?" he pursed his lips.

"Because," she rolled her eyes, "I'm pretty sure I can't do much rolled up in this." She held tighter onto the red sheet.

Julio cast her a salacious glance; his laughter infectious. "Considering what I'm thinking you won't be needing that."

The atmosphere changed.

Angelica scrunched up her small nose and suddenly grinned. "You're impossible."

He shifted on the bed. "Flattery can go a long way."

Seeing him with barely a slip of cloth fettered her X-rated vision. She released her held breath with a hiss. "Is that what this is...flattery?"

"The best kind," he assured her quickly.

"Well, flattery will get you absolutely nowhere," she couldn't help but add.

"If I recall correctly," he patted the bed, "it got me somewhere." She held his inky blue eyes in silence. His ebony eyebrows pleaded as he inhaled steadying air.

All of a sudden, she was hot, needy, and hungry all over again. Her traitorous body started responding in all the obvious places.

He sensed her female pheromones being released. His pupils dilated in response. She parted her lips. The air became thin, stifling.

"I want you," he told her boldly. He came around and let her sheet fall. It puddled at their feet.

He still wanted her, that fact was hard evidence.

She was tempted, oh, how, she was tempted. His mouth took hers to intoxicating moments of rapturous delight. Titillating her five senses.

He pushed her back until her bare calves braced against the side of the bed. If she let go of him, she would freefall backwards. She wrapped her arms around him feeling his arousal against her belly.

Her body hummed to life.

She should push him away, she thought, even as she drew closer to him. How was it that she could want him again?

She swallowed the lump, which filled her throat. Wanting him seemed right. Losing utter physical control seemed right. Together they went down on the bed, and he took her to that same glorious place with him.

It was wild and passionate sending her into a higher level of need to satisfy him. He chuckled, pleased with her enthusiasm. He was frantic for her, and she completely understood. Bolts of red-hot desire consumed her. Julio flipped her over and onto her knees then drove into her with sheer urgency. She expected nothing less because her urgency matched his. And when they found their release it nearly overtook them.

He pulled her against his moist chest until their breathing regained a calm, perfect rhythm.

Nothing was said...nothing could be said. The sex was off the charts. Mind blowing.

Angelica didn't even know how to explain it, or how to accept it. So instead, she gave him a calm, affectionate kiss.

He brushed her hair away from her face and simply cast her his devilish smile. She'd never experienced a moment quite like this. It was surreal.

"Angel," he said.

"Yes," she mumbled against his shoulder, too tired to do anything else.

"I want more of this," he admitted. "Too good to not see what this is."

"Huh?" she yawned.

He watched her eyelids flutter then fall with earnest content. It crossed his mind to tell her then. Tell her that his name upon her left hip meant something to him. That he should've never walked away leaving her to hold the baggage of his selfish discontent. He'd been a damn fool. Would he let history repeat itself? Now that he'd gotten a taste. He wanted more of her. He wanted to peel away the layers determining what made her tick. But when she came and smiled at him, he forgot everything including his own name.

He'd never felt this invested. Sure, he'd been in many relationships before, but emotional attachments never entered into it. He should never have brought her here. Should have never touched her soft, supple white skin. He'd let down his guard. Something he never did. So quickly she'd gotten under his skin.

How stupid he'd been. He knew nothing good ever came in letting people get too close and personal. His mother's shortcomings had certainly taught him to always be on the defense. His mother had suffered at the hands of two men, and he had sworn he would never be like that. A prisoner to love. He'd seen the emotional consequences first hand.

Angelica was the complete package...beautiful, intelligent, hotter than a firecracker in bed. The steady beat of her heart beating, ticking against his chest had made him forget all the anguish that had plagued him.

Pangs of panic driven terror completely gripped him. This didn't mean anything. He was panicking for absolutely no reason. He had slept with other women. They'd enjoyed consensual sex and then moved on with no regrets, he conceded grimly. In fact, only a few more times of this with the world's most beautiful woman cradled against him, he could confront whatever lurked ahead.

She understood him. Had always understood him. She was clever, so clever. In business as well as in bed. He was honored she had succumbed to him. He knew, through the gossip mill, she never let men in and here he was in bed with his sexy little siren.

But for the briefest moment, his fears crashed to the surface spreading like a grass fire into his chest.

What happens next?

Was he being greedy?

What if he wanted to have more than sex?

He pulled her sleeping form closer and shoved those crazed, restless thoughts from his head.

He had no worries because Angelica was as disinterested from anything further developing be-tween them as him. She understood the rules.

Just then she moved, throwing her leg over him. Another urgent wave of need spiraled through him.

He never lost sight of his goals. He followed a rigid game plan with no room for distractions. And Angelica Watson was certainly a distraction. His best-laid plans had considerable holes and that never happened to him.

He'd never let sex go straight to his head. Romance was unrealistic. Fairytales.   He was a damned good businessman, an expert at sealing the deal. And sex was no different. You negotiated the terms. Took pleasure and gave pleasure in return. Formed a full proof deal. No bartering, no promises, and a woman who never delved into his private life. A simple transaction.

Chapter 7

Angelica glanced at the clock and couldn't believe the time. It was mid-morning. She never slept in. Never. She checked the clock again. No mistake, it was half past nine. She shivered as she lay huddled beneath the cool, satin sheets, feeling exposed and vulnerable. She eyed the steady rise and fall of Julio's chest as he slept. If she moved, she would wake him, and when his eyes opened reality crept in. Dang reality.

Asleep he didn't seem so distant, so domineering. The whisper of his breathing was so quiet he seemed peaceful. Almost. She knew beneath that deceptive façade was a heart of steel. A man determined to win at everything. Her stomach churned into a tumult of emotions she didn't think she'd ever be able to solve.

How had she gotten herself in this situation? She was in bed with a man who physically wanted her. Yes, undeniable, and she wanted him. It was awkward to say the least. Last night had been more than a sexual encounter, and although his powerful presence had been impossible to ignore, Angelica had witnessed a man who had lost himself within their physical euphoria but nothing else. What was the matter with her? Hadn't she spent the last nearly two decades eradicating those fanciful memories only to almost concede beneath kisses from a man that already had too much power over her?

Julio opened his eyes to catch her watching, no studying, him. He smiled a clandestine smile.

"That's one of my flaws," he said.

She looked up in surprise knowing she'd been caught. "What?" She tucked the sheet tighter beneath her chin.

"I hate waking up in the morning until I've had at least two strong black cups of coffee."
She shrugged and tucked some stray hair behind her ear. "You mean you have a flaw?"

"Hmm," he paused for a minute. "I'm human after all."

She laid her hand upon his bare chest. "That isn't the rumors I've been hearing."

"Noted," he admitted. "I'm sure there's been a lot of them."

Angelica shrugged, then climbed from the bed, pretending to consider the conversation, but wanting to put needed distance between them. She pulled the discarded blanket around her.

"Maybe," her lips clamped together. Seeing

him propped against the headboard, sheet barely covering his midsection, sent X-rated memories crashing to the surface of her mind. Those kinds of memories weren't helpful at all.

Carefully she made her way to the shower without tripping and falling in her haste. She heard his laughter drifting behind her.

When showered and dressed, she headed from the bedroom to find Julio. The fragrant aroma of coffee was coming from the kitchen. She could hear movement, but when she walked in, the sight of him wasn't what she'd envisioned. What had she been expecting? She wasn't sure but the image of him with his back to her, his feet propped on a chair, a coffee mug cradled between his hands, his olive skin gleaming and dark hair damp, sent a glitch to her heart rate. All of his male gorgeousness was crazy sexy, especially now, she'd had a forbidden taste. He turned and his knowing eyes encompassed her glowing, pink cheeks. He lifted a quizzical brow, "Sit," he poured coffee into another cup. "I've got a meeting today," he said, before taking another sip of coffee.

Angelica accepted the cup before eyeing his comfortable attire. He certainly was dressed down for a business meeting. He looked sublime encased in well-worn faded jeans, blue tee shirt, and sneakers. Her brow spiked with curiosity. "What kind of

meeting happens on a Saturday?" she asked, out-
wardly skeptical.

"You'll see," he finished off the last dregs of
coffee and hitched a gym bag on his broad shoulder.
"Is this about my business," she asked, catching a
whiff of his signature cologne. A heady sensation,
which sent tremors down her spine. "What's up,
Suarez? I'm coming."

"Whatever," he said. "I'm going to be late we
should go. Dress comfortably," he instructed. His
boys were too important. He didn't have time to
argue with her.

Julio placed his hand on the small of her back
and followed her to the lift. His slightest touch was
messing with her defenses. Once in the elevator her
eyes remained focused on the downward acceleration
of the numbers. As soon as the doors slid open, she
scrambled out. He exited at a more leisurely pace.
The parking garage was full of vehicles, he escorted
her to one of his. A short, stout, smiling driver nodded his head and opened the door for her.

"Where are we going?" she wanted to know as
they cleared the garage and entered the city traffic.

"Be patient, querida. You'll see." he promised, his arms folded over his chest, his biceps bulg-
ing beneath the short sleeves of the tee.

Damn, this guy was too hot. He definitely
kept a strict workout regimen. All she had to do was

look at him to start panting with need. Her, love em and leave em, mantra was going to be a hard one to keep.

Now that she'd had a taste of what he had to offer. The physical satisfaction had been beyond great. As far as lover's went, he'd knocked it out of the park. She knew better than to get involved with the man who controlled their company, but here she was deep in the muck.

Her bravado was strong, but she didn't do one-night stands or sleep around with men. As a matter of fact, she didn't have much of a relationship history at all. A few dates in high school and university, but nothing serious, until Derek. And he'd been nothing but a disaster. Sure, she told Julio they were only casual, but were they?

The lingering connection of years past still hampered her thoughts. She'd never forgotten the past. How could she? She'd heard of love at first glance and all that nonsense, but she never believed it. And she didn't now. The newness would wear off. After all, how could she be intimate with a man, who attracted her, and feel nothing at all? Unrealistic. She didn't do casual, and she didn't do intense. So, what was she doing?

Her shield was slipping. She'd thought she was stronger than this. Had her protected heart

weakened? The last few days hadn't been quite
the outcome she was expecting. His come-on had
thrown her for a tailspin. She inconspicuously
studied him. Luxuriant dark hair brushed his collar,
prickly beginnings of dark stubble accentuated his
chiseled jawline and the perfect bow of his mouth,
throwing his high cheekbones into prominence.

　　The ground rules had been laid out. Keep it
simple, no emotions, no feelings, purely sex. She
wanted him, but could she keep it at that? She'd
always been headstrong and rebellious. Simon could
attest to that if need be.

　　Unlike her, Julio had concrete reasons to be
withdrawn and relationship free. What had really
happened? Experiencing what he'd suffered would
give any guy good measure to form boundaries.
Could he ever open up? Would he? His coping mechanism was to push people away. Was he capable of
changing?

　　Tender emotions scared Angelica. She had
trust issues. Her company, her family, were nothing
but a business deal to him. A business acquisition.
He was married to his empire, and he didn't have
room for family. Family, a flutter of hopefulness,
filled her stomach. The image of a black-haired little
boy, or girl, snuck into her mind. The possibility
took root and flourished. Did she want children?

The opportunity to have children had never presented itself.

What did this relationship with Julio really
mean? Lust? She wondered. Something caviled at
her subconsciousness. Anger and uncertainty mottled her brow. Did falling into bed with an attractive
man constitute anything? Had he broken some sort
of barrier? Had the impossible happened? Willing
herself to stay calm, to keep her feelings in check,
she glanced over at him. His single show of vulnerability had demolished her defenses. And now she
had to pull in the ropes and regain a tight leash on
her feelings. Apprehension filled her eyes and dark
smudges shadowed the circles beneath them. Her
sleep patterns had been sporadic over the past few
months with worry over business, family, and now
Suarez. She shivered.

"You cold?" he grinned and placed his hand on
her knee.

"A little," she admitted.

He turned down the A/C. "We're almost
there," he said, his hand massaging her skin.

Angelica shivered again her forehead creasing.
Anticipation?
Attraction?
Fear?
Or maybe all those things.

Angelica's knee tingled where he touched her. She felt his eyes on her, but she refused to look his way. Instead, she looked out the window at the passing scenery. Looking at him made her crave him more than she should. Closing her eyes, she tried to calm her throbbing heartbeat. The heat, the smell of the man made her want to curl in close to him and draw strength and comfort. But there wasn't comfort only more unrest. Still, right now, she couldn't resist him or pull herself away. She wanted more of this... togetherness.

She noticed they'd entered the inner-city. She leaned back and met his gaze and blinked. "What are you up to?"

"Don't look so surprised," his eyes were unreadable. "This is my Saturday gig."

The lot was full of vehicles. They pulled into a parking slot and stopped. People milled about in all directions. Many sporting team emblazoned jerseys. Fans in blue and gold all in full carnival mode. Firecrackers exploded overhead. There was whistling, chanting echoing all around them. Pure mayhem.

"Fútbol?" Angelica looked about her amazed.

"It's the best way to spend a Saturday," he said, releasing his seatbelt and stepping outside. Angelica climbed out into the heat and waited for him to come around. The breeze blew the end of her ponytail into her face. He brushed it back then pecked her cheek. "Come on," he smiled. "You've got a team to meet."

She let him pull her by the hand as they wove through parked cars. His enthusiasm became infectious.

"Slow down, Suarez," she huffed. "I can't keep up."

"Sorry," his boyish grin encompassed her. Suddenly the years were erased, and the billionaire tycoon businessman was replaced with the teenage boy she'd crushed on. The flutter in her chest seemed to flipflop.

"Why the rush?"

"I'm going to be late," he said, "and the guys won't forgive me. I'm always on time, and I never miss a game."

"I had no idea you were such an avid sports fan," she looked at his profile, her pacific-blue eyes filled with a lot more interest than the situation called for.

"You know in BA football is king," he eyed her knowingly. "No Argentinian guy is born without having a love of the game. Before I could walk a ball was placed in my hands."

"Point taken," Angelica's voice told him. "I've even been to a few matches myself."

The place was full, and it seemed all the seats were taken. The hardcore fans swarmed through the gates, filling the terrace. Angelica was hoping she wasn't going to be standing for the entire game. Colorful smoke drifted across the stands. The ground shook with the stooping feet of the congestive mob. Nothing came close to the thrill of an Argentinean football game.

But Julio guided her by putting his hand on her lower back to the side of the field. After several high fives and shoulder slaps from the spectators, he stopped beside a group of boys.

Angelica's eyes widened in surprise. The group of boys surrounded Julio, every one of them talking at the same time. He was in his element; Angelica could tell the boys adored him.

She stood beside him for several minutes, a thousand thoughts and feelings swirling around in her head. "Are you coaching the team?"

He grinned from ear to ear, pride masking his face. "Yeah," he nodded, then gave her hand a squeeze. "Here," he pointed to a bench, "take a seat. Let me know if you need anything."

The competitive environment and the noisy, chanting crowd swallowed her up in the excitement. The game was intense. Julio barked out orders to the kids from the sidelines. Parents cheered and screamed behind the fence; their enthusiasm conta-gious.

Angelica jumped up and down, her throat hoarse from yelling as Julio's team scored the win-ning goal. He picked her up into his arms and swung her around and planted a heartfelt victory kiss on her opened mouth. Passion sparked between them, and her heart flipped. And then something clicked, seeing him with those inner-city kids, melted her heart. The ruthless tycoon had disappeared, and in his place was a man whose emotions had been all over the place. The respect from those boys' eyes cemented her suspicions. Julio's heart wasn't locked up as tight as he wanted everyone to believe. His passion for the kids was evident.

He released her as the crowd surrounded him. He was swept into celebratory embraces. This was a big deal. It was a big win. She waited patiently until he could break away.

Happy bubbles gurgled in her stomach. She was pleased to be a part of his big day. That he had included her in something so personal made her think their relationship might not be so short-lived. Angelica studied the side of his face, wondering if she was making this too big of a deal.

She forced herself to breathe in and out, in and out, to act normal, her heart rearranged itself around the notion of a lasting relationship and family. Angelica's heart cracked wide open. She thought she was immune. After seeing her parent's struggles, she didn't know if she had it in her. Balancing all life's preemptive hardships. Work, love, marriage, family, and some sense of self -preservation.

How to juggle it all?

She swallowed the lump in her throat.

Was it worth it?

She shook her head. She was letting sex and a good experience go to her head. Where was this philosophical questionnaire coming from? Had she lost sight of reality? Julio had already assured her he wasn't in it for the long haul. He only wanted short-term sex. And hadn't she agreed?

He wasn't about her it was about the business.

She had no claim on his time or affections.

She needed to start training her mind to be subjective.

She'd been so used to policing every aspect of her life.

"Why was she faltering?

Panic curled in the pit of her stomach. She needed to leave. She needed to get away from him. Time to think. Analyze her feelings.

Seeing him kick the ball around reminded her of a time long ago on the beach. Of her overwhelming teenage crush. The one she'd thought she'd recover from. However, she still suffered from the afflictions of that short-lived connection.

She had to act now.

If she played her cards right, she could lose herself in the crowd. He'd never notice.

Edging toward the fence, Angelica pressed her way through the milling bodies. Picking up the pace nearly running to her freedom. She was suddenly restless and brimming with pent-up energy.

She could already breathe easier. Mixed emotions flooded her. She was being pathetic. She was almost to the open gate when he clasped her arm. "Going somewhere?"

She smiled, licking her overly dry lips. "I was just trying to beat the crowd," she lied to save face. He examined her facial features, doubt shrouding his eyes. She knew he knew she was lying, but she didn't care.

• • •

Once inside the vehicle, Angelica became quiet. Julio examined her profile, wondering if he'd said, or did, something upsetting her. He thought, he shook his head, he didn't know what he thought.

No matter what he was thinking would be wrong.

Maybe it was none of his business, but he found himself reaching out to her anyway. "You okay?"

She glanced at him and offered up a tired smile. "Yeah. Just a bit tired."

He grinned knowingly. He hadn't allowed her to get much sleep last night.

"When you get home, get some rest. We should call it a day."

She stared at him, the words wrapping around her. He was attempting to let her off the hook. She should be thankful, but she wasn't. "Should we..." She started, then stopped, cheeks flaming hot. Assumptions were the master of all screw ups. How would she feel if he started making assumptions? She thought maybe they would've picked up where they'd left off. She was being foolish to stake any sort of claim.

His steady gaze shifted to her face, and there was definite scorching heat in his eyes. "What did you think?"

Raw, compelling hunger masked his face. He wanted her; the fire was there.

"Nothing," she backtracked.

"What the hell happened back there?" His voice sounded strained and formal.

"I don't know what you mean," she managed to keep her tone light and breezy, covering any hint of disappointment from her voice.

"You bolted," he explained.

"Huh?" She started defensively.

He slid his hand across the seat and covered her knee, her whole body lit up. The car's dim interior cast shadows upon his sculptured face. "Didn't you have a good time?"

She nodded, conscious of the pressure of his hand upon her knee. His fingers rubbed in a circular motion causing shivers to branch out in all directions. "Yes, I loved it. Thanks for inviting me."

He cupped her chin and turned her to face him. "Then what's wrong?" Julio demanded.

"I... didn't want to intrude."

He frowned. "Intrude? What do you mean?"

She realized how badly she wanted him. "You know," she held his gaze, "being part of a team. Being part of something. Something special. Seeing you with those kids," she smiled fondly. "You belonged. I've never seen something so real. Those boys respected you. Adored you."

And I want that.

"That camaraderie." She lost all train of thought when his hand moved up the curve of her knee. Her breathing getting a slight hitch in it. "I've never been part of a team," she said. "I've only had the type of respect that comes from being head of the company, the owner's daughter. You know what I mean?"

"You're right," he said, moving his hand up another inch and stealing the rest of her breath away. "You don't make friends in business, Angelica. Mergers and acquisitions are cutthroat. Business transactions are straight forward, whereas, real life tends to get a bit messier. But coaching those boys on that team," he got a look, a sense of belonging, "we've got each other's back. It gives those boys purpose. Something to look forward to. We're family."

Something passed through Julio's eyes. Pride, maybe, or some other form of emotion. Angelica felt a giant hitch in her heart. She caught a glimpse of the boy he used to be. The boy who'd trudged through life struggling to simply achieve his goals.

Soon embarrassment lit her heart-shaped face. "I'm sorry I got cold feet." Angelica glanced away again, looking at the city lights, disturbed how she welcomed his presence and this newfound security. "I'm not prepared for all this," she looked back at him.

He laughed and once again squeezed her knee. "Don't get so uptight about everything. Let's play this thing out. Let nature take its course. You and I both understand sex."

"Sex is sex, but business is business," Angelica pulled in a deep breath.

"I'm smart enough to separate the two," Julio stated.

She sucked in a sharp intake of air. "I don't believe you, Suarez? This isn't about business, is it? It's about paying me and Simon back. Getting me into your bed was an added bonus. It's all about hurting me," she pulled back. Are you happy? You've succeeded."

"Have I?" His expression didn't mock her as she'd expected and that bothered her more than if it had.

"You've got control of the company," she spouted out loudly. "Simon had a damn heart attack," she pulled in more air, "and I wish I'd never met you." Simon's illness weighed upon her shoulders. It was an additional burden to bear.

His hooded eyes scanned her face. "Do you hate me, Angelica?" One eyebrow arched curiously. "Is Watson Enterprises all that's important to you?" She clenched her teeth together and turned her head. "You don't understand."

He truly didn't understand. She was making too big of a deal out of this whole thing. It was just sex. These rioting emotions meant nothing. But seeing him with those kids had caused her to want things. Seeing his complete dedication and willingness to give a day had touched something really deep that she wasn't ready to label yet.

He was an enigma she couldn't quite get. Didn't understand.

He cupped her cheek and his little half-smile sent heat spiraling to her insides. "Does this mean the wall is back up?"

"It never came down," she said, ignoring the heat his touch was causing.

"Yes, it did." The pads of his fingers massaged the sensitive skin beneath. "A touch tells a person many things.

He was too much of a distraction. She needed to be focused. And Suarez was certainly a major distraction. Wanting him wasn't part of the plan. Keeping involved in the day-to-day operations of the company and formulating a plan to get it back was where she needed to be. She pulled back from his caressing touch. She wanted to be angry, but his soft words and the feel of his breath threatened her common sense the way nothing else could. She had to focus.

The vehicle stopped outside her home. She knew she was being wishy-washy by wanting him, but needing to push him away. She wanted him inside. Hot molten lava flowed through her veins. She wanted to curl her hand around his neck and take more from him. Basic, hotter than hot, lust simmered in her chest. Inviting him in would be crazy, but she couldn't help herself. She looked toward the house. "Come in."

No matter how foolish she longed for the fire of his kiss.

Julio studied her intently, before shaking his head. "You keep sending mixed signals, querida. You and I both know if I come inside how it'll end up."

"How's that?" Her voice came across way too husky and needy.

He laughed and pulled her close. "With me deep inside you, and you screaming my name."

"Oh," Angelica shivered as he kissed her senseless.

He pulled away and left her trembling. "As much as I would like to stay, I've got work to do."

The sting of his rejection hurt. She'd managed to avoid messy entanglements since Derek. How many times had she used her career as relationship intervention? Then why did she still long for the culmination of his kiss?

Chapter 8

Julio had been tied up in business meetings all week. He personally handled the controversary over permits. The final resolutions had been smoothed over. The entire Watson situation was dominating his time.

Somewhere along the way he had tossed out all of his rationality. His mind drifted frequently to Angelica. He'd lost sight of his mission.

Revenge...

He knew it was wise to keep his distance.

He wanted Angelica. He spent almost two decades with a gnawing ache of unfulfilled desire for justice, and she'd haunted almost every single day of it.

He'd been lost at the first kiss.

It made no logical sense. He shook his head momentarily disoriented.

He took the opportunity to have all his basic needs fulfilled.

His need for her.

Renewed desire rushed through him. A golden opportunity had presented itself, and he'd taken it.

He was finally able to satisfy the twinge of lust that had plagued his every sleepless night. Perversely, her invading his thoughts, angered him.

He hadn't thought touching her would set off such a chain of events.

His mind raced, jangled with endless possibilities. He couldn't keep up. Their amazing night of hot sex had drove out logical thinking. Never mind that he had invited her along to the football match. His topnotch statistical, analytical mind hadn't been functioning. He'd missed a couple important details in current business meetings he never missed.

Unacceptable behavior.

He'd lost himself in Angelica's slender, willing arms.

He took a deep breath, then released it. He clenched his hand tighter around the glass, which was pressed in his hand. The smooth amber liquid sent a burning sensation to his empty stomach, but the stout peppery liquor wasn't going to fix this. He massaged his temples hoping to relieve the pressure. Weren't things going according to plan? Seduce her, make her care, ruin her. He owed it to his mother. He hadn't forgotten.

He was disgusted with himself for his lack of resistance.

These days of not seeing her made him restless and on edge. He'd been avoiding her, thinking it would allow him to get a grip on all of his mixed emotions.

He'd mostly tried to ignore the graphic lust-filled images which kept plaguing him.

Damn, if he could get a handle on any of it. Today was the anniversary of a day he tried to forget, his mother's death. He was wallowing in self-pity. A human emotion...he tried to bury beneath layers of thick skin. It wasn't like him. Things like this, he kept close to his chest, not making a big deal out of the occasion. No big surprises for him. Wasted time and energy. Tonight, he didn't want to be alone, instead be with Angelica who somehow plagued him. Desire lifted, its languorous presence inside him. Julio grabbed his leather jacket, and headed out the door. He didn't want her, yet he did.

• • •

Angelica hadn't seen Julio for the last five days, and now he showed up at her door. She knew he'd been busy tearing her company apart. Julio was very astute and, as she suspected, he knew things to do to accomplish the end results.

Oh, my---when she saw him it took her breath away. Absence hadn't changed a thing. He had the power to unnerve her. He was dressed in black from head to toe. He was wearing motorcycle boots. The sight of him dressed so sexy shot electrifying heat straight to her unmentionable regions. She was torn between being happy, or unhappy, to see him.

She was not going to let him waltz in and out on a whim. She wouldn't be a booty call for any man.

She weighed her options.

"Get dressed," he said, his brow quirked, eyeing her cat purrfect pajamas.

Displeasure pleated her brow. She pulled herself straighter and threw back her shoulders. His face was dark, inscrutable. She shook her head at his outrageous demands. She wouldn't be controlled or told what to do. No way. His audacity was almost laughable. He surely didn't expect her to comply.

She lifted her head. "No, I am dressed. What are you doing here?"

He stepped closer. "Looking for you."

"What for?" she asked, seething with building anger. "I'm not in the mood to deal with you. We're not in a boardroom."

He caught her around the waist, tugged her against his body. "No, we're not," he said. "Must you always fight me?" He bent his head and kissed her hard.

She nearly choked on her own breath. He twined his fingers into her hair, then smiled that devilish smile of his. "What do you want?" she sighed, shoulders slumping when he released her. Behind him sat his bad boy motorcycle against the curb. "That's yours?"

"Yes," he said, his lean stubbled jaw, tousled hair adding to the image. He tossed the bike a brief glance before spearing her with his bluest stare. "Do you want to take a ride?"

The thought of sitting behind him, on that machine, with the vibrations humming between her legs created all sorts of thoughts. Delicious thoughts. She didn't know what to think about him. He was certainly full of surprises. It was one of the things she secretly admired about him. She never knew what to expect from him. He made swift, sound decisions, and closed on billion-dollar deals every day. However, right now, his long, powerful legs encased in black jeans, and his black shirt polished off with leather, caused the air to hum with vibrant, radiant energy. The red-hot tycoon looked like a rebel.

"I've never been on a motorbike," she eyed the sleek machine doubtfully. "You can't expect me to climb onto the back of that thing."

His sheepish grin was captivating. "There's a first time for everything. It will make you feel like you never imagined. It'll change you forever."

She nearly choked choosing to ignore the double entendre. "It's late, Suarez. Where are you going anyway?"

His twisted smile wasn't at all cordial. "Curious? You want to go. Get dressed," he ordered.

Angelica threw him a combative glare and her breath shortened as he followed her in the door. She found it very unnerving, the way he was watching her. He took a seat, crossed his ankle over his thigh, dominating her living space. The large airy room suddenly seemed small and confined. She'd forgone any feminine frills or decor. It was sleek, modern, and fitted with oversized furniture. Julio, with his jaw tightly clenched, shrunk the expanse of room with his presence. The scent of his cologne drifted in the air making her long to touch him. His jaw clenched a little tighter, and she sensed something was bothering him.

"I'll get dressed," she told him.

He was pacing when she joined him. She didn't figure she needed anything fancy so she'd dressed in jeans.

When he saw her his eyes lit with appreciation. She shifted under his scrutiny. He reached out and clutched her hand, his dare-devilish, blue eyes locked on hers.

Outside he helped her with the helmet, clasping the latch beneath her chin. Angelica blushed, then looked away, hiding the effect his touch had on her.   He climbed on the bike and indicated she take the seat behind him.

Angelica compressed her lips together and was suddenly nervous. The powerful red machine roared to life, and the rapid vibrations sent quivers along her spine.

"You ready?" he yelled above the noise. She nodded, clasping her arms around his middle feeling the rock-hard solidness of his abs. It took her a little bit to adapt to the sway of the machine. The sway of his body.

The wind in her face, cradled against the man who made her body feel all kinds of things, was super exhilarating. Her heart pounded from the adrenalin rush.

She lost all her inhibitions.

Julio wove in and out of the traffic. Headlights winked at them as they passed by. Angelica had never felt so free in her life. She threw her hands out to catch the breeze.

Arrows of moonbeams filtered through the night sky silhouetting their outlines. She held on tighter wishing she could bottle this feeling and capture it for life. Everything else disappeared as they cruised along the streets. They were the only two people in the world. All the cares and worries suddenly dissipated, almost forgetting they were enemies. It was only her, Julio, and the humming machine.

She never, ever wanted to stop.

Julio did stop. He pulled alongside the curb by the waterfront.

The milonga, or tango hall, had a long line of people, but Julio was escorted right in. The night-life scene wasn't Angelica's style, but Julio seemed primed for the excitement. She'd been to tango salons before but in an exclusive part of town. The city was dotted with these halls where Argentines went to socialize and dance. The room smelled of mildewed brick, sweat, and overpowering clouds of sweet perfume. The ceiling was low-hanging, and the darkened room was windowless. She clasped his arm while several girls eyed her enviously. Pride swelled within her chest that he'd chosen her to partner him.

The crowd was claustrophobic. Bodies were meshed together in cloying pods. The atmosphere crackled with the tedious capacity. The music was loud. Nothing could be heard above the deafening beat.

He led her to a private alcove with several lounging seats. Pillows were piled in a haphazard fashion around the space. Two ceiling fans moaned and creaked, circling hot air to no avail. When they were seated, he ordered drinks. She dropped her bag beside her and waited for him to speak.

"I didn't want to be alone tonight." he raised his voice to be heard above the loud din.   Her brows drew together. "Why me?" she asked, her mouth, pink and full. "You haven't phoned, texted, or had any contact with me." She was frowning. "What changed your mind now? I'm certain you can pick and choose," she looked around the room at the scantily clad women, "any companion you want." He lifted his dark eyebrow, sensing her jealousy. His lips split into another alarming smile. "It's you I want right now," he said flatly.

His slow, measured words sent a flicker of awareness straight to her limbs. A satisfactory smugness settled into her heart. Seeing him again set her on fire. Hungry desire was ever present in his deep-set gaze. Knowing he was barely containing the fiery heat made her feel all tense inside.

She slowly sipped her fruity drink to help slow down her hormonal fluctuation. Simply put, she was hot and bothered. Suddenly her mouth was bone-dry even with the cool drink splashing against her tongue.

They were locked into a stalemate. Alpha vs alpha.

Angelica wasn't a pushover. If he thought he

could waltz back in, bat those sexy silvery-blue hypnotizing eyes, and she would be panting.

Then he was right.

"Do you go clubbing a lot?" She was having a hard time imagining this was his usual scene.

"No," he was quick to reply.

The dance floor was filled with people. Angelica scanned the colorful inhabitants. The couples danced well, but sinful. Her gaze landed on one particular pair. The man was sporting sleeked back, oiled hair, pierced eyebrows, and a round belly. His partner had endless legs, and voluptuous hips with her dress front split down to a bejeweled naval. He twirled her, slotted in pirouettes, and leaned diagonally nearly tipping to one side. It was tango without staunch rules, which was all she'd ever seen. She turned back to Julio, curious why he brought her here.

"Then what's the occasion?" She pressed her lips together as if she was patrolling him. "What are we celebrating?"

A shadow passed over him and the glint in his gaze hardened to steel. "Not celebrating, forgetting."

Angelica raised a surprised brow. Instant compassion filled her susceptible heart. That Julio, emotionally controlled Julio, could feel such vulnerability. She put down her glass and laid her hand upon his and squeezed. "Do you want to talk about it?"

He couldn't hide the tension that filled him. The taut lines etched into his cheeks. "No, not necessarily."

Julio was determined to overcome the grief assailing him because he refused to be weak or vulnerable. He had years to perfect his nightmarish memories. He'd built an empire. He'd overcome the weakness.

Angelica looked into the faraway, haunted vividness of his startling blue eyes, and her heart clenched as if clamps squeezed it. She sucked in a deep breath as realization dawned on her. "Oh, no, Julio. Is this the date...?" She couldn't say more.

"Si." His jawline was stoic and his expression became bland. Stone cold and emotionless. His deadpan eyes revealed nothing.

She wanted to comfort him. She squeezed his hand again. "I can't imagine your painful suffering. Please..."

"I don't want your pity," he jerked his hand from beneath hers clearly telling her to keep her pity and concern to herself. "It was a long time ago, a tragedy that shouldn't have happened."

She swallowed the knot clogging her throat. His eyes were haunted. Brooding. Bleak. She licked her dry lips. "Julio?"

He looked at her, annoyance stamped upon his face. "What?" He made no attempt to hide his impatience.

"I know what this is about, Suarez. The company, the stock, and you and me." she said, knowing the answer. "Stripping me down until there's nothing left."

He stiffened, and she knew she had the answer.

"What did you expect?" he spat out.

She nearly choked on her drink. "Until a while ago I was the head of a major corporation. Your senseless vendetta won't stop me from fighting hard for Watson Enterprises."

He looked at her his cold stare revealing nothing. "Tonight, isn't about business or vendettas, but forgetting." He reached out, trailed his fingertips down the front of her shirt, her nipples snapped to attention, his fingers rolled over the tight nub. "Let's dance," he said, tugging her to her feet. In his arms she could feel the simmering anger of his body heat. The crowd parted to allow them into the jammed space. Bubbling tension shrouded their entwined bodies. When he twirled her across the floor, she met him step for step. They danced until she was out of breath and sweating. And then, the grinding music stopped, and the tango began.

Angelica swiftly stepped away, but Julio swung her back. His hands clasped her hips. And all the passionate dance moves had culminated at the apex of his powerful thighs.

He danced like magic. His precision was precise and controlled. She was a novice in comparison. He carried her along. He closed the space between them. Their bodies were aligned in perfect symmetry. He wanted her. She could feel it in every fiber of his being. It was obvious.

The crowd stepped away. It was only the two of them. He was so good her mistakes weren't noticed or seen. She met him step for step. Beat for beat. Her heart was racing with exertion and compelling passion.

She'd never tangoed with such vibrance, the sensual language of dance.

Her head was spinning.

At the crescendo he kissed her. God, how he kissed her. All his pent-up emotional demons. Her lips parted, and his tongue delved deep within. They were fire and ice. Desperation exploding within them. It was wild and passionate, and yet, so basic. He laughed, a guttural laugh, in that infuriating way of his.

Her heart sped away with the burning hunger he'd induced in her quivering limbs. The wolf whistles and clapping finally brought logic crashing back into the cocoon surrounding them. The jeans he wore did nothing to conceal his arousal. Piercing hunger kicked deep between her thighs. All of a sudden, she was hot, needy, and wanting him all to herself.

He leaned his forehead against hers and whispered. "Here's the situation," he paused to catch his breath, "I know you want me, and tonight, I need you."

She didn't say a word. None were needed. They grabbed their stuff and nearly ran from the room. Outside the building he pushed her against the wall and crushed her lips. She ground her hips against his.

His Spanish curses mirrored her need. Her hands were all over him. Their frantic desire was simply crazy.

"Not here, querida. Not here."

She sighed. How could she have forgotten they were in public? Her body was humming with unrequited pleasure. Embarrassment colored her cheeks. She was behaving like a sex-starved madwoman.

He affectionately caressed her cheek. "Come on beautiful," he eyed her with glittering wicked eyes, "I know a place we can go. It's close by."

The bike ride was short and sweet. He parked along the pier. She eyed him quizzically.

"Camila is moored over there." He pointed to a sleek, luxury yacht bobbing in the water.

"Your boat is named after your mother?"

He shrugged his shoulders. "What of it?" he snapped. "She meant a lot to me."

It saddened and delighted her that he was willing to confess this simple little thing. Him sharing it with her meant something.

Several boats were scattered in the harbor like fall leaves floating on a pond. Waves slapped rhythmically against the sleek hull, and in the distant shoreline, scattered lights twinkled like holiday magic. It was a beautiful boat, not the sleek white style of so many of the monstrosities she had seen moored in the bay. Although, it was modern, it had the classic ambiance of an old black-and-white film. It was more than a hundred feet long, and the main salon was at deck level. A sweeping line of numerous portholes suggested fitted cabins below. It's natural wood trimmings, polished wooden deck, brass lamps under canopies added to the charming look. A fitting, classy tribute to his mother.

He moved past her and helped her onto the shiny deck of the floating palace. He wasted no time taking her across the space and down the steps.

He tugged her along with him not really giving her time to really see. The bedroom had a ridiculously large bed. "I want you," he told her boldly.

His hands curved her hips and pulled her into him. How could she resist? "Suarez," she began.

What followed was wild, passionate, and provocative just like their dance.

"Do you want me?" He moaned with need. She released the front of his jeans. The tip of his arousal pressed against the heat of her core. No words were needed, her body answered him. She was determined to avoid anything serious between them. It was best to keep walls built. But she desperately, urgently needed to feel him.

To touch him.

She assuaged her conscience by convincing herself he needed this. That he needed to be held. She was bringing comfort to his hurting heart. That their coupling would somehow bring him peace. Right. Try telling that to her big, stupid heart. It was starting to become crazy about him.

He was frantic for her, and she was frantic for him.

"This," he murmured, "this is what I've been craving. God, I missed you."

Their kiss was fierce and hungry leaving them both gasping as they fell onto the bed. Clothes scattered wherever they landed. Where his nude body ended, hers began.

He slid on protection and drove into her with urgent force. It wasn't unexpected. His exorcism of all those painful, unhappy memories was driving him.

"Oh...my...God...Suarez," she gripped his shoulders and rode out the storm with him.

The explosive release nearly overpowered both of them.

She was too sated to even move or breathe.

What had just happened was pretty extreme.

He cracked an eye open. "Are you okay?"

Complete silence surrounded them. Seconds ticked by.

"Yeah," Angelica murmured, wrapping both arms around him. "More than okay."

His eyes closed, then popped open again. His jaw hardened. She could feel his invisible shield surrounding him. "I'm glad," he said simply.

She idly ran her other hand along the richness of his stubbled jaw. Slowly the dark cloud that had ridden roughshod over his head all night long began to reappear. The pain in his face was evident. She wanted to console him and make that pain disappear, but she didn't know what to say. Angelica raised up on one elbow and looked down at him. She realized she was falling for him all over again.

Chapter 9

Angelica woke the next morning finding Julio spooned against her backside. She shivered as the late-night recollections came crashing in. He had made love to her over and over again. Every muscle in her body was screaming from the exertion.

She knew Julio had shown her the most vulnerable side of himself. Last night he'd been insatiable. His breathing was deep and even. His hand was placed against her ribcage just below the curve of her breast. She shivered with longing.

Their non-committal relationship had turned a sharp corner, and she knew it. She couldn't resist him at all.

He groaned and his stiff growth of whiskers were abrasive against her cheek. His hand moved upward and teased her protruding peak. He brushed her hair back from her forehead. "Good morning, querida. Are you hungry?" His tone was soft, but she sensed the undercurrents. "I'm starving. Surely there's food somewhere on this thing."

He climbed from the bed and threw her his wicked grin. He wasn't one bit embarrassed about his nakedness or the fact she couldn't take her eyes off him.

The magic had gone, and cold reality was settling in. A sense of apprehension wafted over her as she studied Julio's tousled black hair and nude body. Her past, present, and future fears were suddenly given life.

"Shower?" he said, and reached for her hand. She clasped it and followed him into the bathroom. Opening the glass door, he pulled her in with him. He tested the temperature by sticking his hand under the spray. His hunger pangs swiftly changed directions. He kissed her soundly then stepped out the door dripping wet. Angelica heard him rummaging through a draw before he stepped back in. He rolled on protection with one hand and pressed her against the shower wall with the other.

He knew he should take it slow, but urgency consumed him. Resolve filled him, and an unwanted emotion grew and took root. She was getting under his skin. His carefully thought-out plan had become more complicated than he suspected.

He needed to tell her. He had to tell her.
She was going to be mad. Mad as hell.
But the timing just wasn't right.
He wasn't ready to lose her...or this.
He drove into her with one slick stroke mak-

ing them both gasp with pleasure.

She would find out sooner or later and when she did, she wouldn't accept him. Everything he had done was for a reason. Instead of a boy, he'd be the man, who crushed her hopes and dreams.

She wrapped her legs around his hips and opened her eyes and stared deeply into his.

"This is so special," he said as he slowed his pace, driving in and out, the languid strokes driving the intensity to the moon. "We fit together so well," he sighed. "No matter what happens, understand we can't fake this."

Christ, why was he groveling and drooling all over her feet. He knew when she found out the truth, she'd never look at him the same way again. Angelica's response was a loud, unladylike gasp. She couldn't answer him.

"This is too good not to last," he said, as he picked up speed, their combined breathing patterns growing faster.

She cried out her release, dragging her nails down his broad, slick back.

He let go too, throwing his head back, closing his eyes, the splashing water cascading over their heated bodies.

She wrapped her arms around him, and he held her until she could breathe.

Julio made no immediate reply, channeling the thoughts in his head. His eyes rested on her. How incredibly beautiful she looked. A mythical goddess with all her slick, wet hair flowing down her back. Resolve filled him. He had to let her accept what was happening between them.

But when she looked up and smiled at him, his air got caught somewhere deep within his chest. His mind went blank, and he forgot everything including his own name.

He had to focus.

He leaned back and closed his eyes for a second. He needed to end this. Whatever this was. He didn't want her breaking barriers and getting too close. He'd let down his guard, and he didn't like it. She made him feel things he swore he would never feel. He wanted to hammer a wedge between them, but he wasn't ready to let her go. It seemed a bit fickle but he wanted to experience a closeness with a woman unlike he's never had before. He deserved a "normal" day before ending it for real.

He wanted more, for a day anyway.

Over breakfast, on the sunny polished deck, Angelica was relieved he was talking about ordinary things. She wasn't ready to discuss intimate stuff. Even though a lot of that had been going on.

"It's Sunday. Let's play hooky," he smiled

mischievously. "What would you like to do today?" He took a sip of orange juice and waited for her answer. "Do you want to take the boat out?"

He waited tensely, wishing and hoping, she didn't deny him.

Angelica loved the water, but boat rides tended to make her seasick. She shook her head. "I'd rather not," she told him regretfully. "I get sick. Apparently," she laughed, "I don't have the stomach for it."

His voice, when he spoke, was serious, if not surprised. "I didn't think anything phased you." "You thought wrong because bouncing around on unruly waves gets me every time."

He saw her eyelashes flicker, and then she smiled. Julio was glad. "The bike then? "Let's take a daytrip. Do you want to?"

"Sure," she agreed. Angelica didn't want her time with him to end quite yet. She liked this relaxed version of Julio. Lighthearted and fun-to-be-around side of him.

Hours later they were driving along the flat, rolling countryside surrounding Buenos Aires. It had been so long since Angelica had left the city. Particularly since the financial downturn her life was in. This part of the country was populated with tons of estancias. Cowboys on horseback tended the cows as they passed by.

The fresh air, sunshine, and present company made Angelica feel giddy and carefree.   And she
hadn't felt like this in a long time. Maybe never.

She had to grow up quite early. Her life had
been full of structured schedules and events. She
was a workaholic, and she knew this. Her relationships couldn't be labeled romances.

Julio pulled alongside a small cafe. The quaint
building had mounds of colorful flowers surrounding the outdoor tables. The scent from the colorful
vegetation dwarfed around them. Hanging his helmet on the handlebar, he offered her his hand as she
climbed off to join him.

"Something smells great," he said cheerfully.
Angelica settled herself on one of the wicker chairs
with a pleasurable sigh. She couldn't ask for a love-
lier day than this. Julio was being so attentive. His
chiseled, handsome face, as he sat across from her,
made her sigh.

The food was simple but delicious.

Angelica sat and listened to Julio chatting
about all the places he'd been. Since they'd both
seen so much of the world, they both could relate.

He leaned back and wiped his mouth with a
napkin before he spoke. "If you could choose only
one place," he asked curiously, "one you could see

again or never been, where would it be?"

She looked at him from beneath her lashes and shook her head. "I don't know, why?"

"Curious," he said, shrugging his shoulders. "There's surely someplace."

She rested her chin in her hand and tapped her fingers against her cheek. "Oh," her eyes got dreamy. "I've always wanted to stay in a quaint, thatched roofed, English cottage with a stone fence, and roses blooming everywhere. I would sit in front of the fire on a cool, chilly night, eating crumpets and drinking tea."

He threw back his head and laughed, the sound was infectious. "I thought you would choose Paris, London, or New York City."

"Nope," and he could hear the warmth in her voice, and smiled.

His eyes looked bland and serious, but she could see the humor in them. "The whole English cottage thing leans a little toward romanticism to me. I thought you would stay clear of that."

She wrinkled her nose at him. "Inside every girl lies a fairytale."

He simply smiled again. "I suppose you like rom-coms and chick flicks?"

She slapped her hand on her chest and laughed. "I'll never tell."

In fact, she'd spent many nights, home alone, watching that exact thing wishing, in her heart, she could find the real thing.

Could he ever be her thing?

An unknown emotion welled up in her middle as she sighed.

They had driven down miles of flat country roads with her arms wrapped around him on the motorbike. He'd even stopped once and let her give it a try. Amidst trial and error and a shaky start, she'd finally drove them several miles. Of course, his hands sliding up and down her ribs and clutching her breast, distracted her many times.

"Caray," he laughed good-naturedly. "I wasn't sure if I was going to survive," he said when they changed seats.

"It's your fault," she threw back. "You should've never trusted me to maneuver a motorcycle."

They took their time and meandered along the countryside. Neither in a hurry. Pointing at the cows and horses as they ate in the pastures. They had stopped and took a break walking hand in hand along the fence line. They talked about mundane things, but no business, and nothing serious.

They found a huge shade tree, and Julio cradled her in his arms as they took a short siesta.

Relief was utmost in her mind. Having him this way, so relaxed, listening to her every word, and not judging her in any way. Oh, she was still very much aware of his magnetic pull. The awareness that sparked between them from simply a touch or a look. But instead, they didn't pursue it right now, they just enjoyed the day.

She felt far removed from the complications that muddied their everyday association. The things ingrained into her seemed so far away. That he controlled her business, her lifeline, was a dead point. The very idea caused her stomach muscles to clench in pain. Angelica forced her mind to veer from that train of thought because it would ruin their absolutely perfect day.

She didn't want to cope with it right now. It was simpler that way. Spending time with him was becoming easier with each second. Right now, she only wanted to continue enjoying this glorious day.

As they headed back toward the city, Julio's mood darkened with each passing mile. The trip was silent. Only the roar of the bike surrounding them. He was restless and short-tempered as he thought about the woman sitting behind him. Angelica kept blindsiding him. A myriad of emotions was bombarding him. He didn't know exactly how to identify what he was feeling.

In all his life; he'd never experienced such

a wonderful day. He'd never let any woman into his personal domain. Nor, his inner feelings and thoughts. But somehow, Angelica had got him talking about his dreams and ambitions. His barriers had accidentally been broken. He didn't want to share those things with her. He'd taken her to the damn football game. Since his mother, those kids were the closest and dearest things to his heart, and he'd revealed it to her. Was he losing his mind? What had happened to making her and Simon pay for the suffering in his life? The sorrow and pain. The vision of his mother, lying on the floor. A gut-wrenching pain coiled deep within his gut. All this time, he'd withheld his emotions and covered his pain. Why now? And with the woman he swore to resent.

Had he become soft? Weak? His mind was clouded with tortured thoughts.

The sex was mind-blowing. Off-the-charts great.

No other woman had made him feel that way in bed. His body craved hers, the more he touched her, the more he wanted. His past sexual encounters had been noncommittal, unemotional. Fulfilling his basic needs. But this was different. He couldn't quite put his finger on it.

He wanted to take her away to that little English cottage she'd described and spend days having his way with her.

No outside interferences.

The image of her bare body wrapped around his sent his libido into overdrive.

His body ached for her.

Julio sped up needing to get back to the city. He mustn't lose sight of what he set out to do. Bring the Watson's down. He needed to subdue his lust for her, finalize their business, tell her the truth, and get the hell out of her life.

Angelica knew the moment he'd thrown up his instant shield. She ought to because she'd done a master class on it. She could feel the renewed tension in his muscles and see it in his clenched jaw line. As evening fast approached, so were the shadows of doubt.

For a woman who had vowed to never let another man enter her heart again, there he was chipping at the edges. She felt sorry for him. She gripped him a little tighter wanting to somehow comfort him even though he didn't want it. Holding him helped her understand him a tiny bit. Made her almost forgive him for how he treated her when he had walked out and now walked back into her life. He pulled into his underground parking garage and backed his bike into the tight slotted space. She handed him her helmet as he hung them into place. Her eyes were searching his, looking for any indication of what had caused his mood to change. Although his lips resembled a smile, the sentiment never reached his eyes.

She dropped her eyes and turned her face away so her blatant feelings wouldn't be so recognizable.

Julio deliberately let the moment pass. His voice was cool and casual when he spoke. "Did you enjoy yourself?"

"Oh, yes," she said, turning back towards him. She started to say more but hesitated. Her eyes searched his face. Her every instinct springing on high alert.

"Thank you," she said, her voice low. "Today is absolutely what I needed. No pressure, no responsibilities, just relaxation." She reached up and briefly brushed his cheek.

An instant flare of longing sprung into the intensity of his eyes. "You must know I don't often do things like this. As a matter of fact," he stated, his eyes hooded, "I never do this."

"Well," she smiled brightly, "I'm glad you did."

"Angelica, there's something you need to know," he started, as he headed for the elevator. She held back, calming wayward emotions. He was hot, then cold, leaving her second guessing her decisions.

She knew that if she went with him, something in this non-relationship would change.

She wanted to break away, run actually. Yet, that volcanic flurry of hunger forced her feet to quickly follow him. There was something about an elevator, once the doors closed, he pulled her to his chest and kissed her. The humming vibrations surged through her blood sending sizzling awareness into overdrive again.

She clung to him. He could arouse her like no other man before him. A single touch and she was trembling with need. She was thirsty for him. She couldn't get enough of him.

Angelica was certain if there had been windows in the enclosed steel they'd been fogged over. The panting going on was absolutely crazy.

She pushed on his chest and stepped back. She needed to come up for air. The elevator dinged and the doors slid open. His penthouse was shrouded in darkness, moonlight casting spears of light. Julio flipped the lights on revealing his mussed hair and askew shirt.

Her cheeks pinkened, and she tried to look at everything but him. This was getting out of hand, not being able to be near him without wanting him. Did she have an off switch?

"What do I need to know?" her eyes held his with singular intensity.

"I've made a decision," he said, because that was the simplest answer.

"When?" she held her breath knowing she wasn't going to like it.

"Recently," he paused. "I've decided to dissolve Watson Enterprises."

She nearly choked, her heart racing at breakneck speed. "What?"

"Surprised?" he shrugged. "You knew it was coming."

"We need to work together? And now this?" She leaned back against the door to support her balance. "What about my employees? What about me?"

"There will be options, financial compensations, and help with obtaining other employment," he offered as explanation.

She kept her gaze locked on his face. "So," she paused, her heart aching, "that's what all this is about? Hurting me?"

"No," he replied coldly. "It's not about you. It's business."

"Really?" She didn't believe him. "Go ahead, punish me, but not them. Our company owes the employees our respect. Our loyalty."

He studied her intently. "I owe it to myself to make sound business decisions. In my opinion, this is it."

"I can't sit back and let this happen."

"I'm in control, Angelica. The choice is no longer yours to make."

It was the bitter truth no matter how unwilling she was to accept it. She knew she was unable to stop his forward progress no matter how much it hurt.

"Do you think destroying me and Simon will fix anything? Bring back Camila? I'm sorry," she said softly, "I truly am. You say it isn't personal, when in fact, it always has been."

Angelica bit her lip and held his annoyed gaze. Her gut clenched. He thought she was a pay-back, a conquest, a means to an end. He didn't need her business. "What's your plan for me, Suarez? Fire me?" The hurt in her eyes was evident.

"Believe what you want," he said. I don't know yet."

"What about us?" she said, suddenly this manipulative game was too much.

The heat in his eyes was unexpected. One look Into their obsidian depths and her heart clamored. "Commitment and happily-ever-after aren't my thing, but I like having you in my bed."

The words sounded so emotionless. But she'd fell into his bed knowing all the bullet points beforehand. It'd been no secret. Today had proven they were compatible, but not feasible. They'd grown closer in some ways.

But there was one huge, whopping issue.

She had fallen in love with him.

The heart followed its own business plan.

How foolish she'd been to fall for him? He would never commit. He just said as much. No promises. No declaration of love. No future plans.

She turned her face away; not aware she was frowning. He smoothed the crease from her pleaded brow.

"Say it, querida?"

She pulled her gaze up to his. How in the world did she explain it? "What are we doing, Julio?" The question floated between them.

"What do you mean?" his voice sounded clipped. Restricted. Darkness shadowed his face. She pursed her lips together.

The ensuing silence lingered between them.

"I mean, what is this?" the words came out softly. Her entire body tensed as she looked at him. "I'm feeling a bit overwhelmed."

"Does there always need to be an explanation." He scraped a hand through his hair, irritation scowling upon his forehead. "Why do women always want to label things?" Something about his question seemed jarring. Constricted.

She'd hit a nerve. "Julio...?" She approached him, touching his forearm. She couldn't push him, that she understood, because she wanted so much more with him. It was a fine line balancing making love to the man who was dead set on punishing her. She squeezed her eyes shut but that had no effect on halting her mounting feelings.

"What do you want from me?" She shook her head. "To roll over and pretend what you're doing is ok? Go ahead," she swallowed, a lump forming in her throat, "tear apart the company, fire me, do what you're going to do, but you don't own me, Suarez. "And," she added chillingly, "me in your bed was a mistake. It's stopping now. Goodbye, Julio," she shouldered past him and headed toward the door.

The tension in his face was encapsulated. He gripped her arm, a deep-seated feeling choking him. "This is far from over, Angelica." His eyes searched hers as if he wanted desperately to find the solution in their cool depths. "I still want you," he snapped out a warning in Spanish. "I'm in control, querida. Do you understand?"

She drew herself up to her full height and sucked back tears which burned the back of her eyes. She pulled her arm away as if his touch scorched her. "Not this time, Suarez," she forced a laugh, hiding the threat of moisture welling near the surface. "For once I'm in control."

Julio didn't know how long he stood there staring at the empty doorway. She was right, for once, she did have the upper hand. The irony of it all. The sweet taste of revenge...it's what he'd dwelled on for years. Controlling Watson Enterprises. Making Angelica want him. Seeing Simon destroyed. So, why didn't he feel like he'd won? Instead, he felt like he was losing miserably.

Cold conviction thickened his bloodstream. He knew what he had to do, perform an exorcism. This had to stop. This borderline obsession with Angelica. Resisting her was getting harder and harder. It was time to take her to the beach where it had all begun and draw that damn line back in the sand.

Chapter 10

The first rays of daylight were casting their colorful hues over the Buenos Aires skyline, but Julio barely noticed the difference. It felt like a lifetime had passed since he'd seen Angelica rather than only an expanse of a few hours. He hadn't slept much and his blurry, reddened eyes showed it. He'd sat in the damn chair all night letting his mind torture him. He missed her sweet body like crazy.

Julio was restless and on edge. He tapped his phone screen, checked his emails, replying to the ones that needed immediate attention. He scrolled through his texts, then called his PA and cleared his calendar for the day. The only good thing in this whole mess, he thought, was he owned and controlled everything that mattered to Simon Watson.

He'd tell her that Simon deserved to suffer.

A seed of doubt ate at him. It pricked his chest and pitted his middle.

Was it satisfaction that gripped him? Or was it something else?

Julio arched a black brow and a sneer curled his upper lip. The emotional strain was beginning to

take its toll on him. He needed to make her understand his position. How could he explain to her what
he couldn't explain to himself? The waters were
muddied with so much debris he couldn't see past
the murkiness. Exhaustion washed over him, and
his shoulders were imbedded with aching pain. He
rolled his head to release the kinks and rubbed the
back of his neck.

He sucked in a deep, fortifying breath. He'd
left her before, and he would do so again. She would
hate him. He leaned his head against the back of the
chair, his eyes closed, then snapped open again. He
needed to end this. He didn't need her chiseling
away at the ice surrounding his heart. It was now a
black hole. He exhaled a long, deep breath, and the
forced air gushed from between his lips.

She didn't understand him.

He never meant for Angelica Watson to get to
him, but she had.

He shoved the thought away angrily.

He was on the brink of losing control, and he
didn't like it.

Something hot and sharp stabbed the back of
his eyes. He fought the burning sensation from deep
within. He couldn't imagine not holding her, kissing
her, and whispering promises he couldn't, wouldn't,
keep. He was a hypocrite. He would be deliberate

when he told her. He had planned it for so long. His insides felt like they were splitting into pieces. He'd only felt this way once before. His mother's death. Would Camila want this?

His penchant for revenge?

No, his mother had a kind soul, and she wouldn't have approved of his unscrupulous tactics. It was on him, but he was justified in his reasoning. His jaw hardened.

He was growing soft like his mother. Look how that ended. Sure, his body craved hers, needed hers in fact, and he showed no indication of tiring of her. Every time he made love to her, he wanted her even more. Yet, he couldn't lose sight of his plan. Ruining the Watsons' had gotten him through his darkest moments. It had given him the drive to be here today.

He would knock down every wall she'd erected. The time was now. His heart had absolutely no influence over him, he decided. He would prove Angelica was nothing more than a strategic bargaining chip.

Angelica stood inside her door knowing Julio was on the other side. Her heart was in noncompliance with her mind, unruly and beating frantically. It was doing funny little hops, jumps, and skips. His Spanish lilt became more pronounced when he was agitated. A little twinge of longing hit her as she pictured his incredibly sexy smile and other sexy parts of his anatomy.

"Open the door, Angelica. I know you're in there." Julio pounded again. "Listen, mi vida, we need to talk."

"I've nothing more to say to you. Go away!"

"I'm not leaving until you open this door."

Angelica chewed her bottom lip. She knew he meant it. "I've said all I want to say," she insisted. "Leave me alone. Please."

"Angelica, I'm warning you---open the damn door or I'll..."

"You'll what..." she jerked open the door removing the wooden shield between them, "kick it down? I'd like to see you try," she hissed.

His eyes glittered with annoyance. "I would have."

Angelica stepped over the threshold forcing him to back up. She wasn't about to let him in. "What's so important that you would've knocked my door down?"

She placed her hand on her hip and glared. False bravado. The sight of him with hair mussed, eyes red, and his jaw unshaven made her heart flip-flop within her chest. Although he continued to threaten her sanity, she wasn't at all immune to him.

Right now, she couldn't quit thinking about all the passionate encounters they'd shared.

Her continued obstinance set Julio's temper on edge. Something about Angelica's standoffish demeanor got his attention. And kept it. The only good thing in this whole mess, he thought, was his quest to destroy the Watson's was coming to an end. Soon Angelica would never want anything to do with him again.

Isn't that what he wanted?

It felt like a vise-grip clamped onto his heart and squeezed, but he ignored the pain.

He cupped his hand around her elbow and pulled her near him. "I have something to show you then you'll understand."

"Haven't you done enough, Suarez?"

"No, I haven't," his gaze raked over her, pausing too long on her lips.

His deliciousness was doing crazy things to her sanity. Angelica wanted to toss caution to the wind and throw herself into his arms while ravaging his mouth.

"What more could you have to say to me? Haven't you tormented me enough?"

He pushed his hand through his hair, blew out a sharp breath, then sighed. "This talk is long overdue." He held out his hand. "Please, Angelica, this once will you do what I say?"

She heaved a sigh, then clasped his hand. "Fine," she said softly, her throat parched and dry. "Let's get this over with so I can get on with my life."

Because God help her, mending a broken heart would take some time.

Julio pulled Angelica along behind him. The helicopter sat waiting atop the helipad of the rooftop of his penthouse suite.

The sky had many shades of orange and pink. The rooftop view was like a picturesque postcard and so awe inspiring. His hand was placed on the arch of her back where it met the top of her derriere. Julio longed to caress her sun-kissed skin but knew if he touched her now, they would never leave.

He opened the chopper door and helped her get into the seat. He went around to the other side of the cockpit and climbed in.

She arched her eyebrows with surprise. "Are you flying this thing?"
He kept his gaze fixed on Angelica as he flipped switches and prepared things. "Yes," he said. Her eyes widened.
"Seriously?" she asked. "Are you certain you know how to control all of these?" She pointed to the dashboard with complicated gages, switches, but-

tons, and things.

"I'm an expert pilot," he said, while pulling the straps to hold her in.

"Is it far?" She placed her hand on his forearm, then snatched it back just as quickly.

"You'll see," he said, averting his eyes to keep from responding. He checked that all the controls were full and free. He cranked the engine and engaged the rotors; the copter's whirring sound was almost deafening. He placed a headset over her ears and gave her a thumbs up as they started lifting from the pad. Without headsets, hearing each other above the din of the spinning rotors was impossible.

Angelica had ridden in helicopters before, many times, but the intimacy of the two of them together was entirely different. She captured his eyes, then adverted her crystalline blue glance, their communication was filled with mixed signals. As they took flight, Angelica took in their surroundings.

Here, under the canopy of clouds, the view was amazing. She briefly closed her eyes as they left the city skyline and flew over the dots of greenery. Her heart hummed with the rhythm of the huge machine.

She was curious of their destination, but she didn't ask. He seemed distracted.

"We're almost there," his voice popped through the headset as they began their slow descent.

She nodded. The short flight hadn't taken long and without incident.

When he landed, her heart nearly stopped beating within her chest. Sadness washed over her. This place she'd never forget. Pelican Cove. A place she'd vowed to never visit again.

The Watson family's old beach house.

Angelica's heart buzzed. She was trying to make sense out of it. Hurtful memories and anger filled her. She hated this place.

As all the noise died down, Julio kept his gaze fixed on Angelica. A sharp, knowing glint appeared in his eyes. He could see the confusion on her face as she looked around. The familiar surroundings had the needed effect.

He reached across releasing the apparatus holding her in. His hands working of their own vi-olation, he reached into her hair and pulled her lips against his. As his tongue darted against hers, their breathing increased.

She yanked back.

"Why are we here?" A hot blush of color stole over her cheeks. She searched his face for answers, but his expression remained inscrutable. "Simon and I left this place a long time ago," her voice hardened. "It's best left in the past."

He shrugged his right shoulder before releasing himself and exiting the machine. She didn't wait for him to come around before opening the door and meeting him on the ground.

"Come on," he said, and headed toward the house.

Angelica dug in her heels. "No!" Deep pounding heartbeats echoed in her ears. "I'm not going in there. "What's this about?" A sour taste filled her mouth. "Take me home, Suarez." His eyes remained expressionless. "Who owns this?" she bombarded him with questions.

"It's mine," his tone had a commanding edge, which made her stand her ground firmly.

"Damnit, Suarez! I'm leaving right now." He made no effort to acknowledge her, even when she caught up with him.

"Suarez," she shot him a look of annoyance. "What's going on? Why did you bring me here? This is…," her voice halted as he held up his hand.

"Inside," he ordered. "Then we'll talk."

When she stepped inside the door, although the interior had changed, memories, sad memories, came crashing in. This was the last place they'd been when her mother had died. The last place she'd been when the young, brokenhearted girl had

to grow up. The place where Simon had left her
with caregiver after caregiver while he tried to fill
his empty void. This place had caused her grief, but
more than that guilt.

Her body responded physiologically.

She froze, her heart began to palpitate. The
rapid staccato pounded within her chest. Desperation constricted her throat. The four walls were
closing in around her. She felt faint. Julio caught
her elbow when her legs began to shake.

Perspiration clung to her brow, and he could
see the paleness of her skin. "Are you okay?" His
brow furrowed with instant concern. "Sit down
while I get you something to drink."

She sat down and bit her nails while he
brought her some water.

The cool moisture eased the sick hollow in the
pit of her stomach.

She made no effort to acknowledge him, even
when he stood beside her.

She placed the glass on the table as her panic
attack began to ease. It had been a long time since
she'd even thought about this place. In fact, she
didn't think about it at all. It held too many bad, bad
memories.

"When did you buy this?" She pressed, cloying hurt filling her throat.

He smoothed his hand through his hair and then turned away. "A long time ago."

"I don't understand," she said, questions in her eyes. "What are the chances?"

He turned back and knelt down on one knee. "It didn't happen by chance, mi amor. I bought it for my own selfish reasons."

"That doesn't make a whole lot of sense." She searched the blue depths of his eyes. "What selfish reasons?" She leaned forward rubbing her forehead. "Tell me."

He pulled back and clasped her shoulders in his grip, massaging the deltoid muscles. The gentle circular motion eased the tension. She closed her eyes savoring the feelings it was creating. Even with his arrogance she still wanted him. Her lashes fluttered open anticipating his intent. She moistened her lips.

He didn't disappoint, their mouths fused together in a hard, savage kiss. His expert mastery simply made her forget all time and space, her mind hazy with repressed desire.

Sliding his hands down to the curve of her hips, Julio deepened the intensity of their kiss. The imposed abstinence, from her, caused his blood to feel sluggish and thick. He kept telling himself again and again that he must end this addictive sexual relationship. His rising anger was targeted at himself for not being able to resist.

"It's okay, Julio," she said, as she held onto him as he tried to slip back. She wanted, no needed, for Julio to make love to her and bring some form of semblance to all this nonsense. Angelica needed the added reassurance. She pressed her lips into his neck feeling the heavy thumping of his heart beating there.

"Angelica, I'm sorry."

It was taking a while to catch his breath. He knew what he had to do. It wasn't fair to take continued pleasure from having great sex. Although she was willing, and he was able, the end result wouldn't change anything. It couldn't be helped; they were both going to feel the distress. But with her breasts pressed up against his chest, his body refused to follow his mind's demands.

Angelica knew they were at an impasse. She could feel it disintegrating. Yet, she refused to let go. This house was a bad omen. If walls could talk, she shook her head. She buried her nose into his neck. "I don't want safe words and broken promises," she moaned against the hollow of his neck, "I just want," she paused a catch in her breath, "the fire. Please, Julio, give me that..."

He picked her up and her legs wrapped around

his waist. He cupped and squeezed her bottom and kissed her hard upon the mouth. Her plump lips parted giving him free and easy access.

There was no time for steady and slow. Their clothes flew off, then he carried her to the bed. Her fingers groped him and his arousal nearly burst through his pants. It was always like this between them. There was no denying that. Every time they touched, pandora's box of savage passion came spiraling out. It was unexplainable; the ignition of fire that blazed between them.

He parted her thighs and thrust straight into her molten heat. She gasped and panted, her nails biting deep into his back. He drove faster and deeper until nothing else mattered except reaching the culmination of the orgasmic pleasure they were both seeking. She met his fast and furious pace, screaming his name as brilliant color exploded between them until they were both spent and collapsed.

It took a long time for their racing hearts to readjust themselves. Angelica bore his weight as they lie together in an entwined heap of naked, entangled limbs.

He rolled off her, and she propped up watching the slowing of his heaving chest.

"Why are you through with me?" she asked softly.

Color heightened his cheek and he tried to

look away. "What do you mean?"

"Don't play dumb with me, Suarez," she countered back. "What did I do," she laid her hand upon
his warm chest, "to deserve this? The brush off, I
mean."

Julio clenched his jaw and breathed in slowly. "Don't psychoanalysis me." He hopped up out
of the bed, nude and glared down at her superb body
splayed out before him. "You knew this was coming.
You knew it would end."

Pain embedded deep within her chest. She let
all her fears and insecurities take root and surface.
The overwhelming feelings were like a weight upon
her chest. Weighing her down into an abysmal re-
cess. She got up, gathered her clothes and put them
on to divert his eyes from her distress. She looked at
him, the burning behind her eyes mounting with her
distress. He stood before her powerful, unclothed,
and seemingly not caring. She forced her mind to
disassociate from the six pack abs and everything
attached to them.

"Is this what you always do, Suarez? You
push people away. Use them?" She snarled at him.
"I guess I'm not surprised, men of your caliber are
known for it."

He finally tossed on his jeans and eliminated
the distraction he presented. "I warned you that I
didn't do relationships. We agreed to remain logical

and sensible about all of this. My work is my life and your life too," he stated, crossing the room, looking out the windows at the crashing ocean below. "It's better this way. To just end it. With no complications." He turned back and eyed her seriously. "I didn't get where I'm at to let anything interfere with it."

The trouble was, she had distracted him from business. He continued to make stupid errors. Errors that could jeopardize his livelihood and career. Cold malice filled his stomach. He would never fall into that trap. Love and commitment. This mission for revenge had taken a serious turn in the wrong direction. Angelica had taken full possession of his mind and body. He was obsessed with seeing her, touching her, making her happy.

He had to end this. Before he lost everything, including his heart.

"Don't ever think you know what is best for me," she emphasized. "This time we've spent together was nothing but sex for me." She watched the anger fill his eyes. "Don't look so surprised, Suarez, you're right I'm like a well-oiled machine. You were only a means to an end," she added rudely. "My business means everything to me. Why not get the world-class Julio Suarez as part of the bargain? All is fair in business, wouldn't you say?"

Smugness filled her silvery blue eyes. Good, she thought, she'd riled him.

His eyes hazed red. He walked toward her slowly and stealthy. She stepped back. She could feel rivulets of anger emanating from him. But when he got in front of her, he wrangled his uncontrollable feelings and snatched his shirt off the floor and pulled it over his head.

"Well, there is far more than you understand," he threw out. "You want to know why I bought this beach house that you hate so much," he laughed sinisterly. "I loathe Simon and I resent you," Julio told her then, his voice hard and his midnight gaze pinning her down. "You're the prize, Angel. Spoils of war. The prize is winning. The money I invested is just a way of keeping score."

Anxiety filled her chest as her eyes found his. Angelica felt sick. "I know," she admitted.
Julio locked his grave look on her.

"Yeah, that's right, my beautiful Angelica," his lips curled, as he cupped her cheek. "I hate this place too and all it represents. Your father destroyed my mother." He let out a hollow sound. What hurts me, Angelica, is you're no better than him."
She forgot to breathe. Misery and pain filled his tortured eyes.

Her eyes flickered once, then twice, as she

created space between them. She lifted her chin, her heart empty. "I can't excuse Simon," she whispered sorrowfully.

He rubbed his hand behind his neck. "I know." His eyes glazed over as if he was in a trance. "You knew my mother worked for him."

"Yes," Angelica said.

"Before I turned eighteen."

She waited for him to continue, the silence deafening. A cold chill filled her.

"We had nothing," he raised his gaze, "nothing," he reiterated, tossing his hand in the air. "That's why all this seems so very tempting."

A frown marred her face. She was struggling to understand.

"My father died and left us destitute. You know the story," he said. "My mother," he turned and looked at her for effect, "had an affair with Simon."

"What?" Doubt filled her eyes, and she adamantly shook her head. "That never happened. You're wrong," she said, all her defenses rising.

Her ashen expression gave him cause for concern.

"It's true," he continued. "Ask your father if you don't believe me."

She shook her head, numbness filling her chest cavity. "Simon has shortcomings, I'll admit, but he would never..."

"Fraternize with the help," Julio interrupted, his laugh harsh and unforgiving. "My mother fell for him. I tried to talk to her." He rubbed his brow with his thumb and forefinger. "As soon as I understood the dreadful mistake she was making."

"This house?" she questioned. "Why did you buy it? What did you have to gain?"

His lips curved into a bow. "Ironic, isn't it?"

An all-consuming sickness filled her stomach.

"What's ironic?" she said wistfully.

"Simon had to sell this, along with many other assets. Watson Enterprises has been in the red for a long time, Angelica... But you knew that. I went away to school sad and broken," he swallowed, before he continued, "but I was determined to reach a level of success so I could buy out rich and pompous men like Simon. Privileged men who took advantage of disadvantaged women."

"You're lying!" She covered her ears with her hands. "I don't want to hear any more of this."

"Simon used my mother, then fired her. I tried to help her, but it was useless." His bronze cheekbones hardened. "Depression destroyed her." He shifted closer and lifted her chin so she had to look at him. "Do you know what it's like feeling helpless, Angelica?" Raw emotion crept into the hollowness of his voice. "What's ironic," he said, "is that I met a girl on the beach. That beach," he turned, and pointed out the window. She looked out at the sand and cold dread filled her. "I wanted to hurt you, you see, the way Simon was hurting my mother and me."

Confusion was stamped upon her brow. "I've always known what kind of relationship this is." She didn't smile, but met his eyes with empty regard. He wished he could numb the pain growing in his stomach. He had to make her understand. He had to explain the huge gulf that lay between them. All the reasons, although he craved her like mad, they were so wrong for each other.

"I poured my heart into your hands." He placed his hands on the window ledge, his shoulders tense and aching. "I told you things I had never shared with anyone."

His mind reverted back to that day on the sand. The day when his world had turned upside down. When he'd left Angelica standing, stupidly shedding tears for him. He'd become an orphan and had to grow up and become a man.

He took a calming breath. He'd made stupid, stupid mistakes. But he'd toughened up and used his street smarts and his brilliant, analytical brain to overcome mountains of obstacles that had plagued him.

He walked away from Angelica once, and he

must do it again. His mind must be clear, precise, and clutter free. And when he was with Angelica, his mind and body drifted to forbidden things.
"I found her," anguish mottled his face as he continued. "My mother, lying face down, blood pooled around her head. It was ruled suicide, and I wasn't there." He turned his face toward her, cool, granite resolve filled his eyes.

Smoldering silence permeated between them. Whatever lies Angelica had allowed herself to believe, he soon dispelled them. Julio, the golden boy who'd broken her heart. The teenage crush she'd relegated to history. The one she thought her love alone could save and fix.

"I knew you targeted us all along," she said, her blue eyes void of all expression. "You maliciously crushed my heart way back then. And now," she dug in, remorse and hurt tangible in her voice, "you came back and tried it again. You're despicable, Suarez," she hissed. "If history has taught me anything it is never, ever to trust men." Color flared into her cheeks and her words were laced with venom.

"Because of Simon?" he asked.

"Yes, and someone else."

Jealously sliced through him. Imagining Angelica with someone else upset him. "Who?"

Hurt filled her eyes. Julio didn't like it. "I was young. Impressionable. You changed that, Julio."

He had the sudden urge to smash something.

"Derek was smart, sophisticated, and exponentially driven." She bowed her head. "He used me. Simon placed him in my path. He thought Derek and I would be the answer to his problems." Her hands trembled, she clasped them together. "Financial intervention, but Derek was a con, and full of lies. He seduced me and shattered my trust. "How do you think you're any better than Simon? Derek? You used me for sex and your own selfish plans."

His eyes narrowed into hard, cold slits. Julio seethed with fury. "No. Don't ever compare me to them."

Angelica pounced, wanting to hurt him.

"You're just like all of them."

"Love is a stupid emotion," he laughed cruelly. "My mother died believing in all that. It's pathetic. I've learned that you have to go after what you want or need. I knew I never wanted done to me what my mother experienced. I knew I had to claw my way to the top," he shrugged. "And if I had to break hearts to do that," he eyed her unapologetically. "But everything I've achieved I did by myself, unlike you who was born into it."

Unmitigated fury boiled to the surface of her chest. At that moment she hated him and everything he represented. "I'll pay you back every cent of your money. Don't you worry about that. I want nothing from you ever again." She gritted her teeth to ward off the threat of tears. "I never want to see you again!"

She strode away without a backwards glance.

But as her footsteps hit the sand, she began to falter.

Her insecurities and fears came crashing to the surface. She watched the ocean waves building and cresting, rolling onto the sand. Sitting down, her arms hugged her knees as the water broke covering her toes with the wet granules.

Bitter misery curdled deep within the pit of her belly. The raging fury dimmed within its peak. Here, looking down the long stretch of deserted beach, streams of tears flowed down her cheeks.

He had grown into a man who was unrecognizable from the boy whose name she'd tattooed on her hip. Tonight, he'd shattered her dreams, of the one memory, she held dear to her heart. The time spent with the boy on this very sand.

She looked up at the seagulls dipping and flying in no certain pattern. She wiped the last dregs of wetness from her face as her anger began to dissipate. He wasn't worth it, Julio Suarez, fretting, crying, and worrying her brain.

She tried to make sense of all that was said. She would confront Simon. Sure, Angelica knew after her mother's death, Simon had found solace in various women, then gambling, and lord knows what else. But to be so heartless to cause Camila's death. No, she would never believe it, no matter what Julio said.

But as the ocean played its ominous song, her thoughts were climbing with panic and desperation. Foolishly, she had hoped her and Julio had a chance. That the feelings they shared, in and out of bed, were real. Cemented with emotions that had grown and bound them together.

What a fool she'd been.

Exhaustion flowed through her. She'd fought so hard for her business and now it no longer mattered. Was this sham of a relationship what she wanted? How could she have missed so many important factors to this whole equation? To be so headstrong, strong-willed, and a whiz in business, she'd failed so miserably.

When she let emotions take over, she failed to excel. And excelling was the one thing she was so very good at. Now that she'd had a taste of him how could she let him go without a fight? Because even after all he'd said her shattered, broken heart still wanted him.

The painful tentacles ripped through her. Oh, the pain. The misery. The fragility of her battered, beaten heart as the depth of her love for him finally came clamoring to the surface. She had deceived herself. He simply didn't love her, worse, he used her for revenge.

She wished she could hate him, make the pain stop. Maybe it would be easier to endure.

She hugged her knees to her chest, no longer caring that she was soaking wet. And her tears unleashed themselves in a sobbing, weeping mess.

Julio picked up his pace on the white, sandy beach, when he spotted his Angel with her head bent down upon her knees.

Perspiration beaded upon his skin. And tinges of angst pierced his chest.

He inhaled and exhaled, taking long, deep breaths, hoping to settle the disjointed feelings he was afraid to examine.

On unsteady legs, he stepped over and bent beside her.

Other than a hiccup and a sigh, she ignored his presence.

He knew it was mad, but he wanted to comfort her.

Silent, tense moments passed before she turned her face upward toward him.

His heart broke in two within his chest.

Her eyes were red and swollen. Moisture saturated her cheeks.

She was right, he was no different than the men he accused of doing the same thing.

He'd hurt her. Hurt her bad.

How could he forgive himself?

"Please, don't cry," he muttered, as his voice cracked.

Her turbulent blue orbs matched the motion of the water. She wiped her nose with the back of her hand, before her face crumpled, and the waterworks started all over again.

Julio wrapped his arms around her and held her tight as something hot and sharp burned at the back of his eyes.

She clung to him, until her tears were spent.

She pulled back from him.

Julio sat frozen.

Her eyes were vacant, void, and held nothing as she looked at him.

His stomach muscles knotted with a vengeance.

"I'm sorry it had to come to this, Suarez. The fact that I'm in love with you makes no difference," she explained calmly. Too calmly.

He held perfectly still because suddenly it all mattered to him.

Hardness infiltrated her eyes.

"I won't live like this."

She took her finger and drew that proverbial

line in the sand.

"You stay on your side, and I'll stay on mine," she told him.

As the sand shifted and faded. Julio watched the foaming waves erase all traces of the line away.

Chapter 11

The return journey was harder than she could've imagined. The terrible pain made her feel like she was suffocating. She thought about making her own way back to Buenos Aires, but knew by the time she made the arrangements going back with him would make more sense.

He didn't talk to her, and she didn't talk to him.

Her emotions were ping-ponging between hurt, anger, and humiliation. She had walked straight into this understanding the consequences.

Her entire life had been full of disappointments. She should have never let so many people dictate her decisions. She'd excelled in business but not in her personal life. She should've set her own precedence and moved forward.

She'd held onto the incidental flashbacks in her life instead of reclaiming control and digging out of them.

Her anger had lessened to simply a simmering ache. Love had done nothing but cause her immense pain again.

As soon as they were in the helicopter, she'd purposely put a barrier between them. She reached for the headphones and channeled in some music so she couldn't hear him.

The flight seemed endless, when in actuality, it went really quick.

Sure, she loved him. She hoped it plagued his every waking moment. A metaphorical ghost haunting him. She didn't want to be here. The truth was, she didn't want to be anywhere near him. He'd used her, and it hurt terribly.

He cast her looks several times, but she continued to ignore him.

His jaw stayed clenched and his knuckles remained white as he talked to control to obtain their flight coordinates.

When they landed, she sprung from her seat, as he reached for her hand, intending to say something.

There was nothing left to be said.

He'd severed all hopes of fixing this tedious relationship.

High on the rooftop of the luxurious tower he called his own, Angelica felt very sorry she hadn't found an opening to penetrate his cold, bitter heart. He was the epitome of a rich, lonely man.

"I'm truly sorry, mi amor," he mouthed softly.

"Take care of yourself. I won't bother you again."
And then he was gone.

And just like that Angelica's fragile heart shattered into tiny pieces.

. . .

The next morning, Angelica sat facing Simon, blinking at him across a mound of paperwork that littered her desk in Watson Enterprises headquarters. He'd gotten out of the hospital, but needed to take it easy.

They were on the brink of collapse. The common denominator, Simon.

She looked around the room, which soon would be gone. Another Julio Suarez acquisition. Her personal mementos littered the shelves and a potted plant filled the corner. Sunlight filtered through the shaded window. This had been her second home for so long, she didn't know anything else. Leaving her company wouldn't be an easy thing to do, but crucial.

Her eyes were red, and her face terribly pale. Her night had been miserable. She'd paced the floor with very little sleep. It showed. Her mind was cluttered with emotional overload. She couldn't seem to switch over to the off button. Everyone had troubles, but she'd had more than her fair share. She wanted to be immune, but all this hurt had blindsided her. She'd thought her self-control had been cultivated. Tested. She had felt confident in her ability to step away from hardship, resilient and untouched, like a residual ball bouncing back.

"You've got some explaining to do Simon, and I don't want to hear any of your lame excuses. Why is Suarez doing these things?"

She stared long and hard into Simon's face, willing him to give her the answers.

"You know how it was back then, Angel." Simon shifted in his seat.

"How was it, Simon? You caught up in your own misery," she paused. "Leaving me to suffer in silence."

Simon's mouth opened, then closed again. No sound came out.

No one was smiling now. Angelica's face was marred with grief. She should have ousted her father from the board long ago, and controlled her own destiny. But she hadn't.

Then Simon spoke. "First off, Angel, don't you dare take that tone with me," he said, smug satisfaction filling his face. "What have you done?" He jammed his fingers through his gray mane, his question accusatory. "Ruined everything?"

"What are you talking about?" her eyes narrowed.

"Suarez," Simon snorted. "I wanted to breach his defenses." He continued to look at her. "I knew he was ruthless, but I was banking on his attraction to you."

"I was humiliated then and I still am," she snapped.

I'm sorry, Angel," he reached up and rubbed the back of his neck. Remorsefulness covered his face.

Angelica looked deep into his blue eyes, the same ones she saw when she looked in the mirror. The urge to scream seethed deep in her. "You think I've failed you," her eyes blazed and bitterness laced her tongue. "Your schemes and cons are too much. I've had enough, Simon," she shrugged. "Wasn't it bad enough you conspired with Derek. His lying, cheating schemes nearly broke me. Now, this with Suarez. Sometimes I wonder if you even have a heart," her eyes remained firmly fixed on the diamond bracelet encircling her wrist, avoiding him, mountains of hurt filling her eyes. Her head stayed lowered, "Were you ever capable of being a dad, a husband?" She looked up at him then, her private pain evident, but deep-set anger burned within her. "Do you have any feelings at all?"

Simon's brow furrowed with consternation.

"I want you to understand," he continued. "I cared for your mother. Loved her even. Valere was..." Simon nodded, trying to formulate his thoughts. "I wasn't the best husband or dad. I know that. I tried. I was having a hard time juggling my life back then. I can't expect you to understand." He stood, shaking his head. "I had so many obligations to fulfill."

Angelica's brow furrowed, and she felt sick. "You tried!" She threw at him, years of anger and regret boiling to the surface. "We were your obligation, Simon. Your family."

He began to pace. "But when Valere got sick." He stopped and stared into her face. "I couldn't handle it. I couldn't handle that sort of thing. I was used to money fixing everything." Remorse washed over Simon's face, and his fingers balled white-knuckled in front of him. He felt ashamed. His brush with death had changed his prospective. He'd been wrong. His manipulative actions had caused hurt and pain.

Angelica realized her own hands were clenched in front of her. "Why?"

It all seemed so inadequate.

Simon came back around and took his seat. "I killed my pain with the bottle, then gambling, and women. I foolishly thought I was protecting you," he said softly.

"Ignoring your dying wife and young daughter," Angelica's voice came out terse and venomous. "What the hell was that?"

Simon's head dropped, and he looked down at his lap. "I only wanted what was best for you. For you both."

Angelica laughed, a brittle and bitter laugh. "What I wanted was my father," she said. "A dad who didn't abandon me, then let me spend my whole adolescence thinking no one cared enough for me." Simon closed his eyes, looking older than she'd ever seen him. "You're right," he whispered. "I deserve all of that and more."

"Suarez," Angelica questioned, desperate for all the answers. "You left me blind. I didn't have a clue that Mateo and Julio were one and the same back then." She narrowed her eyes. "But you knew, Simon?"

"Yes," he said simply.

"I was so young," she sighed. "He broke my heart. I can't believe I didn't recognize, Suarez, at first."

"But your heart did," Simon said, swiftly. Angelica said nothing. Her pulse pounded in her neck.

When Simon spoke, his voice cracked with sorrow and regret. "Julio's mother, Camila, took a job in our house. She was so kind and sweet. Like a lost butterfly, really."

"Why?" Angelica wanted to feel sorry for Simon, but hurt and anger still fueled her. She'd been manipulated by men her entire life and from this day forward it would stop. She would take control of her destiny.

He took a deep, ragged breath. "It wasn't supposed to happen. It just did."

Angelica clenched her hands together in her skirt because they were shaking. She tried to make her heart stop racing. "You knew she committed suicide?"

"Yes," his shoulders slumped and his face looked shallow. "I regret that."

"Apparently, she didn't take it that way." Angelica shamefully shook her head.

"There is no excuse for my actions," Simon lamented. "Believe me, Angel, I felt responsible, so I went into rehab."

She remembered when he'd been gone for all those weeks, and she'd been told he was away on business.

"You knew Suarez was the boy on the beach?" she asked, her expression dark with displeasure. "Why didn't you tell me?"

"Trust me, Angel. You were both too young. The two of you had your whole lives ahead." He hung his head. "I can't change the past, Angel. We all have regrets."

The tone he used made her chest hurt. A quiet sadness filled the huge cavity. She'd forgotten the point of all this was saving Watson Enterprises. It didn't matter how she felt. It was Simon's fault. Julio's fault. Julio made her feel things, unwanted things.

"What hurts the most, Simon, is we're no better than Suarez."

Simon snorted. "You're not above repercussions, Angelica. It was your idea to tie Suarez's permits in appropriations. Be honest," he laughed, "you wanted to cripple him. He beat us to the punch is all."

She pressed the heels of her hands into her knees. "Sometimes business is messy," she said brokenly. "Like it or not, it is what it is. After all the warning signs were right in front of me."

"Life is messy, Angel, haven't you learned that yet?" Simon looked entirely too satisfied. "We'll bounce back. We don't need Suarez. His downfall is he couldn't keep his pants on around you. His attitude will change."

It shouldn't have surprised her---shocked her even, the callous look on Simon's face.

"Enough Simon," her tone lowered menacingly. "My relationship with him is not up for discussion. He hates us," she added.

"I've seen the way he looks at you, Angel, and hates not a word I would use to describe it."

"Why did you go to Julio to hedge fund our company? To get us out of the red?"

"Why does it matter?" Simon asked.

"It matters to me, Simon. Doesn't that account for something?"

"I gambled on the chemistry between you two. Can't you see, Angel, it was a full proof solution. The perfect marriage between personal and professional. A bet I had to pursue. Because you're in love with him," satisfaction filled his voice. "Use it to our advantage."

Emotions flooded her system, gushing through her until she couldn't catch her breath. Clogging her throat. "Not this time, Simon. I won't be used as a pawn ever again," she pulled in a ragged breath, her voice sharp and powerful.

"Find your future, Angel," Simon bowed his head. "I'll support whatever decision you make. Go after him," he said, his voice caught with emotion. "Why," she asked, her breath leaving her in a harsh exhalation. "Suarez made up his mind. The choice is no longer mine and I'm in acceptance."

But it hurt, hurt bad.

. . .

Two weeks had gone by and nothing.

Angelica waited for a call or a text, but knew it was her overworked imagination. She hadn't heard anything from Julio since she'd left him after that dreadful trip.

She'd thrown herself into work with a driving vengeance, trying to find a loophole to stop Suarez. But the lack of food and lack of sleep were starting to take their toll and have a lasting effect.

She decided she needed to get away without being reminded of his constant accolades.

Angelica could barely recall getting on a plane or the flight to London's Heathrow Airport. Time dragged by, and the hours seemed endless. She tried to find solace by pouring herself into social media. But her jumbled thoughts kept reverting back to him. Julio's intense blue eyes and smiling lips. And his whispered words and forbidden promises.

Julio had used her.

Simon had used her.

And tricked her.

Julio hadn't loved her from the very beginning.

She had fooled herself into believing otherwise.

But her heart knew no boundaries, and it had picked him to be hopelessly in love with.

Once disembarking from the plane, she used an App to hire an Uber driver to take her to her destination.

Cabbage Rose cottage was aptly named. It was surrounded by a stone fence with roses blooming everywhere. A gurgling stream flowed nearby. Angelica cried because she was standing in front of her daydream.

"Hey, lady you okay?" the Uber driver asked, as he unloaded her bags.

"I'm fine," she said. "A little sentimental I guess."

Angelica hauled her bags into the cottage she'd rented. The eerie quietness surrounded her making her feel desolate and depressed.

She sat her bags on the floor and looked around. The fireplace she wanted was front and center. The comfy little cottage was exactly as described. It was fully appointed with all the amenities she needed. The floral sofas and quaint kitchen were stocked with everything for her stay. She found the bedroom, fresh tears filled her eyes, it was perfect. The iron bed was nestled against the exposed stone wall. Still, her heart felt broken all the same. Now, here she was not knowing how to address her terrible mistakes.

The wounds seemed extremely too deep.

Her phone vibrated, and her heart lurched within her breast. Her deadened hopes took a leap in the air.

She looked at her phone, but it was Simon checking in to see if she'd landed and got settled.

She moped around the cottage picking up this and that.

How could she have been so naive?

How could she have allowed herself to think they had a future when he was unwilling to love her, or want her, like that?

Was she destined to be alone, childless, craving a love she would never have?

What is love? She thought unhappily.

She'd thought her relationship with Derek had been love, but he hadn't even been anywhere close to that.

Her relationships had been lacking in so many facets.

The one relationship she thought had absolutely no merit was the one which carried so much more than that. Most people thought love was a quiet and tranquil entity. Her included. Oh, how she'd been deceived. True love, real love, was so much more. It dug down deep into the fabric of your being. Asking questions, you didn't even know yourself. It was happy, funny, crazy, and distressing. All those things that challenged our true identity. Love was about stripping down all the barriers. Leaving our heart open and bare. There was no protective shell. Angelica had bared her soul, but he hadn't.

Now she had no plan, no direction. Sequestering herself in the family business had never filled the empty void that needed filled. Far from it. It'd been nothing but a smokescreen to hide the true, vulnerable Angelica.

He'd robbed her of the pride, the defenses, she'd so proficiently built. In one, hurtful conversation, he had torn them all down.

Her heart catapulted, hurting so very deep down in her chest.

She closed her eyes, tears tracking down her cheeks.

Looking around she felt a semblance of peace. The cottage, with its carefully tended garden, trellised roses blooming in vibrant shades of pink, yellow and red, and shabby chic furnishings gave her a calmness to face all the rest.

She stepped outside; the stone was cool against her bare feet. It was dark now; the facade of the cottage was shadowed in the moonlight. The roses fluttered in the slight breeze as it picked up their perfumed scent.

She sat on the cute, little wooden bench, and pulled her knees up against her chest.

She didn't know what she would do, but she wanted Julio in her life and in her bed.

But how did you force a man to return your affection?

In the boardroom she'd been known to make outrageous demands, but in the bedroom, she'd never put it all on the table.

And now she sat here in England, far, far away from heartbreak. But running away hadn't given her an answer to any of her questions. She didn't know what she was doing. She didn't even have a simple plan.

The solitude was simply closing in.

She must face the truth and admit he wasn't all to blame. She'd been guilty of driving a wedge between them as well. It was easy to put up walls. She had been so busy hanging onto all of her past pain that she had created a chasm so deep he could've never crossed the crevice.

She hadn't allowed him in. She'd held him at arm's length. She'd made no promises.

The truth be told she'd given Julio every opportunity to push her away.

She wanted him. God, how she wanted him.

But was it the right thing to do? It was dangerous. It was like playing Russian roulette with her life. Could she risk it? Did she dare take the chance?

Rejection burned like fiery whiskey in her belly. Rejection, and the need to feel wanted, had been the bane that bound her all her life.

Would it damage...

Her pride.

Her defenses.

She had to know. It was most likely; if you didn't try you would never succeed.

Perhaps she was more like Simon than she had imagined.

Hiding behind money and prestige.

How ironic it was Suarez's money was financing their monetary needs.

• • •

Julio prized himself on being able to make award-winning decisions, but when it came to his inner feelings he failed miserably.

He hadn't seen Angelica for two, long, grueling weeks.

And he missed her like hell.

He looked like hell.

He should've stopped her. Told her how he felt.

But the problem was, he didn't know himself.

He had only himself to blame.

He'd been a grouch at work and everyone was trying to evade him. He was tossing out unrealistic demands.

A pounding ache vibrated in his head. He tossed back the scotch hoping the liquor would numb the pain in his chest.

How many times had he picked up his iPhone wanting to text her, call her, just to hear her sweet voice at the other end? But he hadn't.

Now the pain, the heartache, were just flowing back and forth inside him, injecting into him like a snakebite.

Had he bathed too long in the sorrow that surrounded him?

Angelica had burrowed herself deep within his thoughts and feelings without even trying. Hadn't she been as standoffish as him?

He had to let the past go. The haunting memories served absolutely no purpose. It had controlled his life for way too many years.

What did he want? What did he really want?

He loved his mother, but she was ruling him from the grave.

He'd never allowed himself those thoughts. He had never gone there. But in this moment, this time, he not only allowed them, he let them flourish and grow. The hazy memory coated him and consumed him completely.

He took another sip of the burning liquid.

He felt sorry for himself. He'd never wallowed in self-pity. It swallowed him until he was ashamed of himself.

Angelica had told him how she loved him in spite of everything. But how could he be forgiven of the things he'd thrown out?

The night sky suddenly looked so very dim.

For only the second time in his life he felt lost.

He had billions, but he felt poor.

Angelica was the light of his life, the shining star.

Without her, the world was off its axis. Spinning all helter-skelter and out of control.

What happened between Simon and Camila had been devastating. It had shaped him. Made him more determined to reach the pinnacle he sat on today. Could he forgive Simon? Yes, for Angelica he would. She mattered that much to him. He finally knew that Angel had been blameless all along.

There was a light at the end of the tunnel. Angelica loved him.

A glimmer of hope lit up his insides. Where there was love, there was hope.

She had to give him another chance.

He would pursue her until she did.

Twice he'd walked away, but this time he was

walking back. Years ago, on the beach, and then; he pushed her out of his life again on the same beach. Hadn't time taught him anything?
She mattered to him more than anything. More than all the money and all the material things.

She was his world. She was his bright and glimmering light.

He'd pushed her away to protect himself. But instead of destroying him she had healed him. He'd found hope and peace within himself.

Peacefulness, brilliant and blinding, flowed through his veins.

He loved her. He loved her beyond reproach. And he'd hurt her, and now he had to ease her pain.

He didn't care about the past. He only cared about the future.

He wanted her without a shadow of a doubt.

He had to marry her, make her his own.

He wanted her more than he could have ever imagined.

His beautiful, beautiful, angelic soulmate.

He closed his eyes, and counted to ten.

He was scared, and he'd never been so damned scared in his life.

Then he knew exactly what he had to do...

Chapter 12

Angelica set her luggage by the front door. She was all packed and ready to go.

Her little dream cottage hadn't given her any reprieve. She'd pretty much spent most of her time in bed, curled up in the fetal position. She'd slept mostly to disassociate from the pain and misery that cocooned her so selfishly. She missed Julio so bad, it burned deep within her chest.

She decided she couldn't stay far, far away sequestered in the English cottage focusing on things that caused nothing but additional pain.

She'd run away from everything, but she couldn't escape her heart.

It was a fickle thing.

She was a fighter, and she would fight.

She wasn't ready to face him.

She spent so many years perfecting her act. She'd forgotten she had a heart.

But it was definitely there.

She stripped her face of all emotion, determined she wouldn't allow any inner turmoil to show. Determined not to acknowledge it to herself. She tucked in her chin, driven, while her eyes glittered with purpose.

She was done with manipulative men.

She gave one last look at the cottage.

It was over with Julio and she could live with that.

She was a woman first, with a strong healthy heart, deep-seated with love that flowed cautiously. She was ready to go home, no matter the price. He wasn't worth the risk.

She had to find the strength to let him go. She'd bartered everything and it wasn't enough.

She double checked again to make sure she'd left nothing out of place.

She was lost deep in her thoughts and her internal resolve when she thought she heard a soft tap on the door.

She paused mid-stride, from her agitated pacing, when there was another tentative rap. She wasn't sure who it could be, she hadn't called a driver yet. The knock got louder, more insistent.

For a moment she wondered if her mind was playing tricks, then she swung open the door.

Julio stood there.

She blinked once… twice… three times to make sure it was him.

It was definitely him.

Every glorious inch of him.

Seeing him sent shock waves straight to her middle.

Was it pain...or relief?

Why was he here?

She wanted to throw her arms around him and cry with relief.

Just when she'd made up her mind, to let him go. Here he stood. For what possible reason? Hadn't they called it quits?

Could she take a chance on them? Her love for him was intact. She hadn't got that wrong. She had decided to be strong and move on with her life. Although, she fundamentally accepted Julio, she'd gained valuable independence.

"Suarez," she said, surprised how calm her voice sounded since her heart pounded erratically.

He stared down at her; his gaze so intense.

He looked frazzled, which was definitely out of place.

She noticed his blue tie was askew and his suit was creased.

"New suit?" she asked, biting her lip, as indecisiveness raged within his gaze.

"Yes," he said quickly, stepping in without an invitation. "We need to talk."

"Sure," she said, meshing her fingers together. Saying mundane, pointless things to hide her uncertainty from him.

The unresolved issues between them cluttered her thoughts. Yet, her senses were full of him. His alluring scent penetrated her nose. The citrusy smell that was such a part of him. Overwhelming sensations bombarded her. Her heart contracted with helpless longing. She wanted to throw herself into his arms because she longed to be there.

Where she belonged.

His gruff voice invaded her reverie. "I'm not here to talk about my suit. I'm here because I want...," he was extremely aware of the rushing flow of adrenalin consuming him, escalating the erratic rhythm of his heart.

"What?" she pleaded unabashedly. "What do you want?"

He didn't answer, his dark hand came up and lifted a blond strand of her hair and wrapped it around his index finger pulling it away from her neck. She shivered with anticipation when his lips whispered against the tender, exposed skin. "You are so beautiful, querida."

Her lungs felt deprived of air, she felt faint.

Julio squinted, emotion filling the blue depths of his eyes. He recognized the unmistakable invitation in hers and relished the brief moment of triumph. He felt all powerful, all male, knowing that she wanted him, that he could ravish her right then and there.

His libido was raging with barely contained restraint.

She was an exceptional woman.

To hell with self-restraint.

He wasn't a saint.

His need to have her overtook his common sense. Then his mouth slammed onto hers as if he couldn't get enough pleasure from her tender lips. She met him all the way, nothing halfway in her reaction.

Combustible energy burst like flames between them.

To gain his sanity, Julio stepped a short distance away.

Swallowing he struggled to catch his breath.

"We need to talk, mi amor." He grimaced, wanting to reach for her and continue his assault on her sensitive flesh.

"I have something for you," he said, handing her a box he held in his other hand.

"What's this?" she asked, reaching for it. The pink box was festooned with beautiful gold ribbons. She opened the lid and found it full of crumpets and numerous flavors of tea. "You remembered," she said.

"I remembered everything," he said. "Go ahead, look a little closer so you don't miss it." He examined the silhouette of her pale skin. She looked so fragile and thin.

Amongst the crumpets and tea lying on a bed of red velvet was a ring. The silver band was graced with entwined hearts and delicately engraved letters J & A. A beautiful, glittering diamond was surrounded by them. Tears of joy pooled in her eyes and slid down her cheeks. A beautiful smile lit her face. Julio knew he'd made the right decision.

"Marry me, querida, and make me the happiest man alive," he knelt before her. "I promise to make you happy for the rest of our lives."

"How did you know where to find me?" she asked, her heart swelling with love and pride, but still needed protected.

It had been a month of heart wrenching reflection. And she was so over it. She didn't want to keep guessing about their relationship. She had wanted answers.

And here he was on one knee proposing to her.

Cabbage Rose Cottage suddenly had become her magical fairytale place after all.

"Simon caved under pressure," he smiled,

running his hands through his hair. He took the ring and slid onto her finger. "Are you going to keep me in suspense? What's your answer?" His smile wavered.

"I've been doing a lot of thinking," she paused, relishing her new found power. "The problem is I simply can't live without you, Suarez," she admitted. "You were my first crush, my first love and my last. You destroyed any chances for future men. But...," she eyed him purposefully.

"There will be no other men," he growled. "But?"

He still held her hand.

"We work together," she quickly tossed back at him. "I will never relinquish my integrity or my independence. We're a team, Suarez, whether apart or together and for every other aspect life throws at us. I refuse to take anything less," her expressive eyes filled with determination.

"Agreed," he said, stroking the pad of his thumb against the softness of her cheek. "I want you by my side, querida, in everything." He kissed her gently. "I'll always be there for you, Angel. I promise."

"We can be happy together," she cupped his unshaven jaw. "I know we can. We've had some great times. Right?" She swallowed, her voice soft and raspy. "Yes. Yes," she said it louder again.

"Yes, Julio Suarez. I'll marry you for better or worse and in sickness and health." She smiled sheepishly, "And until death do us part, even if I give you days of pure hell."

"Hell, with you is heaven on earth," his gaze met hers across the short distance of space. "I'm sorry I turned you away," he proclaimed. "It wasn't your fault all the pain that I felt. I was needing an outlet, lashing out, and you were in my path. When I was a boy, I was too immature to understand, but now, I'd become too foolish, too selfish, and full of myself." He clasped her shoulders, his heart reflected in his eyes. "I love you, my Angel, with all my heart. I was captured by you the first time I laid eyes on you. Although, we were kids, I knew I must have you in the end."

Her heart went tight in her chest and then filled with pure joy. She needed to make sure she fully understood him. "You truly love me?"

"I do," he said.

Angelica wiped her eyes as tears streamed down her cheeks.

"Julio," she said, flinging her arms around his neck and kissing him from his eyes to his chin.

"That's it," he looped his arms around her waist. "You're not even going to make me earn it. Make me beg." He swiped away the happy tears from her face. His heart nearly burst with love.

"Oh, you will," she promised. She looked into the depth of his blue eyes and saw the truth. "I've spent many years trying to protect myself from pain. And then you crashed those barriers, and I didn't know how to handle it. My coping mechanism was to run. I can't imagine my life without you." She slid her arms around his neck. "I love you so much, Julio Suarez. Do you believe me?"

"Not really," he frowned. "I don't deserve your love. I've been a damn fool, and I'll be the first to admit it," he squeezed her tighter afraid to let go. "I believe in love. Don't get me wrong. But the problem is I don't know what a healthy love should look like. What if," he shuddered, "I can't get it right?" She leaned back in the circle of his arms. "Love is about mistakes, Julio, the good and the bad. It's about letting other people into your life. It's about letting bygones be bygones. To forgive and forget." She kissed him fully on the lips. "We can't base our lives on the mistakes our parents made. We both built walls, which we both regret. I love you, Julio. I will say it again and again. I want you. I need you. I want to spend the rest of my life with you." She captured his chiseled face in the palms of her hands. His eyes watered, and she hoped he had truly learned to forgive.

• • •

For some odd reason as Julio stood there on the beach staring at Angelica; he was transported back to the boy of eighteen.

His heart was beating inconsistently.

His palms were sweating.

It seemed like a lifetime, but it'd only been six months, until this day they were to say I do...

Their wedding was a small, private affair.

Nothing fancy.

Just down the stretch of white, sandy beach her father waited along the path of lit tiki lights as dusk began to fall.

The sea of lights gave his Angel an ethereal glow.

She was a vision of loveliness walking bare-foot in the sand. Her wedding dress molding her body, and the white veil blowing behind her in the ocean breeze.

His heart skipped a beat, and he held his breath.

He couldn't wait to take her hands and claim her as his for all eternity.

Simon gave a simple nod and took her hand placing it on his arm as they began their short, slow walk up the aisle of sand.

Music played and the soloist sang, but for the life of him, he couldn't hear the words.

The only person he saw was the woman walking toward him. Tall and strong and full of happiness. Her gaze met his across the space, and even from his location he saw the expression upon her face.

Love. Hope. Joy.

All the years of suffering and pain flowed out to sea with the drifting of the waves.

With every step she took, Julio's eyes couldn't leave her face.

He squared his shoulders and stood tall with pride upon his proud face.

Everything disappeared. All time and all space.

Nothing else mattered.

Except the fierce emotion in both their gazes as their eyes locked and held in place.

She arrived below the arch covered with beautiful flowers, Julio's eyes were filled with intense approval.

Simon shook his hand as he gave her away. Her beautiful smile combined with bright, shining love caused his heart to stall and forget to beat.

"I love you, mi amor," he whispered for her ears alone.

As they exchanged their vows, his heart was full of undying love and conviction.

As the minister pronounced them man and wife, his heart exploded with fierce and passionate pride.

"Hello, Mrs. Suarez." Then he bowed his dark head and kissed her until they were both gasping for air.

The small crowd whistled and cheered.

As they made footprints in the sand on the beach, he twirled her in his arms, and kissed her again until her heart was racing erratically.

As she slid down his chest, Angelica looked up into his face. "I love you, Julio," she whispered softly, the glow on her cheeks. "I'm sorry for taking so long to fully understand. I was scared of rejection. I know our mothers are looking down on us with smiling faces. Thank you for making me your wife today. I couldn't imagine being in a better place."

His bright, loving smile would have melted her cold, icy heart on any day. He shifted her veil from blowing away. "Thank you, querida, for being my heart, my soul, and my wife. I can't imagine my life without you."

"Thank you, for giving Simon and I a second chance." She looked up at him in all seriousness.

"Simon never meant to hurt Camila. You know that, don't you?"

"I loved my mother, and I miss her every day," he shook his head sadly. "I know I should've handled things differently."

She reached up and touched his face. He clasped her hand and kissed each fingertip. "We've both learned our lesson."

"We've all kept our secrets and made mistakes," There were molten blue flames in his gaze as his hold tightened on her. "But enough talk about all that, I've got other things I'd like to be doing to you."

She smiled in agreement, as she nestled closer to his big, strong chest.

He held her hand and ushered her through the sand. Rushing her toward the helicopter on standby to take them to his private jet and off to their honeymoon.

He stopped abruptly causing Angelica to frown. "What?" she fretted. "What is it?"

He looked so serious and solemn she was afraid to ask again.

"Do you love me?" he asked.

She nodded her head.

"Do you trust me?"

She answered by running her finger along his bottom lip.

He shivered and tensed.

"There will be no more boundaries. Do you

understand?" His face smug as he drew that proverbial hated line into the sand.

"No more bartering, no more price to pay, and
no more lines in the sand. It's just you and me. Rec-
onciliation."

He stepped over the visible line drawn in the
sand.

And then he kissed her with all the pent-up
passion from the last two decades since the first day
they'd met....

Epilogue

A year later…

Angelica and Julio were spent.

Bringing their daughter into the world was no easy task. After hours of intense labor, the glorious bundle was put into their arms.

Julio was so proud he couldn't hardly contain himself. The tiny, squirming bundle demanded both of their attention.

He'd never known such joy or happiness. The bond was so intense. He would love and protect these two females with everything he had in him.

He swiped his wife's brow and kissed her cheek. She was spent and tired, but she went through delivery like a champ.

He looked down at the baby nestled so peacefully in the crook of his arm, and his heart swelled even bigger within his chest. "She's beautiful," his eyes misted with emotion. "She's the spitting image of her mother."

"She's also demanding like her father," Angelica's smile filled up the room. They both smiled as baby Suarez found and sucked on her fist.

Julio laughed, the deep rumble vibrating his broad chest. The baby grumbled as he laid her down on her mother's breast. Then she suckled and was soon perfectly content. "You're both amazing," he said. "I can't believe I'm so blessed. I love you both more than I can even express."

Angelica reached up and cupped his cheek. "We love you too my handsome husband. You and our beautiful daughter have made my life absolutely complete."

Fierce pride pierced his heart. "I'm so proud of the life we've created."

And he was. Watson Enterprises now thrived under the Suarez umbrella, which was under the advisement of his beautiful wife Angelica. Julio continued to run his empire with an iron fist, but always took extra time for his family. Simon spent a lot of time golfing, but did his due diligence being a dad. Julio hadn't forgotten his humble beginnings. He still coached the football team. The kids loved him. Together they had created various opportunities for the underprivileged kids. Their joint foundation had provided scholarships, housing, and jobs for the aging-out kids.

They worked together as a team in everything they did.

"What name are we choosing?" he asked, as he put his hand on the soft, downy head.

Angelica sat up, and he fluffed the pillows behind her head. "How about," she smiled softly, "Camila Valere Suarez?"

He clasped her face and kissed her inviting lips. "A fitting name for our perfect family," he agreed. "Thank you, mi amor, for giving me more than I deserve."

Angelica nodded, proud to be all his.

Nothing could be more perfect. He'd torn down the old house and built them a new home on the beach. A place to start their family with no ghosts, no hidden past, and filled with nothing but happiness.

Because his sole purpose was his family, loving and protecting them.

And he did....

Powder River Publishing

www.powderriverpublishing.com

About the Author

Lorine Gray's love of romance, reading and writing, was first inspired by authors like Janet Dailey, Johanna Lindsey and many others. Although, her first attempt at romance novel writing never saw the light of day, her passion for writing endured. She spends her days-and nights-dreaming up steamy alpha heroes and the strong-independent heroines that tame them. Other than writing, Lorine has a passion for restoring and flipping houses, traveling and spending time on the beach. She is the wife of a born and bred Nebraska rancher and mother of two wonderful children. She has also been blessed with four awesome grandkids who she loves spending all her spare time.

www.ingramcontent.com/pod-product-compliance
Lightning Source LLC
Chambersburg PA
CBHW071252190726
48292CB00007B/2511